Joe had been awake for several minutes, lying quietly, enjoying the feeling of having Kitty in his arms, trying not to wake her.

He had no idea if he'd ever get this chance again.

She smelled fantastic. He closed his eyes and breathed in her familiar vanilla scent. She smelled like she felt—warm and soft and sweet. He wanted to bury himself in her. Inhale her, breathe her in, not let her go.

He'd expected her to wake and move out of his arms immediately. He'd expected her to be flustered, embarrassed, affronted, all manner of things but he hadn't expected this. This intimacy, this easiness.

Her hips were pressed in against him. Or he was pressed against her, but as far as he could tell Kitty hadn't noticed. Perhaps she was too distracted by the baby's movements. It was incredible to think that Kitty would be having this experience several times a day. That she had a tiny human growing inside her.

Even though he was doing his best to be supportive, he still wasn't thrilled about the fears for the future that this pregnancy brought up, but he had to admit, he was grateful to the baby right now. If it hadn't started moving he suspected Kitty would have been up and out of bed before she'd even woken properly once she realized the position they were in, but half-asleep and still relaxed, she seemed happy to lie there with him.

Dear Reader,

I've always thought offering to be a surrogate is an amazing, selfless act and have often wondered why women do it. It's a difficult process in Australia due to our legal system, which makes it even more incredible when it happens. I'd like to think I'd be one of those women given the right circumstances, but what are they?

Writing Kitty's story let me explore some of those questions and more.

I hope you enjoy it and if you had a hand in helping me to choose the title—thank you!

I'd love to hear from you if you've enjoyed this story or any of my others. You can visit my website, emily-forbesauthor.com, or drop me a line at emilyforbes@internode.on.net.

Emily

FALLING FOR HIS BEST FRIEND

EMILY FORBES

HARLEQUIN® MEDICAL ROMANCE™

Recycling programs for this product may not exist in your area.

ISBN-13: 978-1-335-66330-6

Falling for His Best Friend

First North American Publication 2018

Copyright © 2018 by Emily Forbes

This edition published by arrangement with Harlequin Books S.A.

For questions and comments about the quality of this book, please contact us at CustomerService@Harlequin.com.

Printed in U.S.A.

Books by Emily Forbes

Harlequin Medical Romance
The Christmas Swap
Waking Up to Dr. Gorgeous
The Hollywood Hills Clinic
Falling for the Single Dad

Tempted & Tamed
A Doctor by Day…
Tamed by the Renegade
A Mother to Make a Family

His Little Christmas Miracle
A Love Against All Odds
One Night That Changed Her Life

Visit the Author Profile page
at Harlequin.com for more titles.

For Sheila.

Thank you for being a true champion of Medical Romance. We couldn't do it without you!

We have had a long association now and I have enjoyed it all, and look forward to many more years, and books, together.

With love and appreciation,

Emily

**Praise for
Emily Forbes**

"*A Mother to Make a Family* is a lovely story about second chances with life and love… A well written, solid tale of sweet love and charming family."
—*Goodreads*

CHAPTER ONE

'YOU'RE DOING *WHAT*?' Mike's eyes *looked* as though they were about to pop out of his skull. 'If you think I'm going to sit here and listen while you tell me you're having another man's baby—'

'I haven't committed to anything yet,' Kitty interrupted, quickly trying to ease the tension. She hated it when he lost his temper. 'I'm just thinking about it.'

'Well, you'd better stop thinking about it.'

'And it's not another man's baby,' she added. She knew she should just keep quiet. Her argument would only serve to fan the flames of his aggravation but if they were going to discuss this she wanted a chance to state her case before this escalated into an argument.

'Is it my baby?'

'Well, no. It would be Cam's.'

'So that *is* another man. If you're going to have babies they'd better damn well be with me.'

With Mike's current attitude Kitty thought it very unlikely that she'd choose to have babies with him but she kept that thought to herself. 'Well, technically it won't be *my* baby either,' she explained, stating the facts. 'I'd just be the surrogate. It will be Jess and Cameron's baby.'

'Why on earth would you want to go through a pregnancy for someone else?'

'You know why,' Kitty stated flatly.

'So, Cameron and Jess get a baby and you get fat.'

'I'd be pregnant, not fat.'

'Still, Cameron doesn't have to put up with the hormones, the weight gain, the mood swings and the cravings but I do?'

'Cameron and Jess have been through plenty already, I don't think you can begrudge them this.' In Kitty's opinion, her sister and her brother-in-law had been through more than their fair share of physical and emotional stresses and she couldn't see any reason why they should be expected to go through any additional stress if it wasn't absolutely necessary.

'Maybe you can't, but at the end of it they'll get a baby and what do I get? A girlfriend with stretch marks and leaking boobs.'

Kitty was pretty sure there was something she could take to stop the leaky boobs and who cared about a few stretch marks if she could give her sister the child she so desperately wanted. The addition that their family desperately needed.

But perhaps Mike had a point. They were supposed to be in a relationship, they were supposed to discuss big decisions like this, and that was exactly what she was trying to do, but if he wasn't going to be reasonable, if he was going to behave like a spoilt brat—well, what did she expect? If she was honest, their relationship was usually about Mike and what he wanted. Their relationship was run on his terms.

Maybe it was time that changed.

Kitty pushed open the door of the Manly Pier Hotel and walked into the pub. After their discussion—Kitty refused to think of it as an argument—Mike had gone out for his regular monthly dinner with his friends from his med school days, and Kitty was relieved that he'd had a prior engagement. She didn't want to continue their discussion all night, but she hadn't wanted to sit at home on her own either. She needed to see a friendly face and she knew she'd find one in the pub that was a favourite among the staff from the North Sydney Hospital and other Manly Beach locals.

The DJ was warming up the crowd. Thursday nights were popular and the place was already busy. She scanned the room.

The crowd was dressed casually but expensively. Kitty hadn't given her outfit a thought. She'd just needed to get out. She looked down at her clothes—jeans, an old T-shirt and canvas trainers. Luckily the dress code for women was never strict but at five feet four inches she felt like an untidy slip of a woman in a room full of glamourous shiny Amazons. She'd pulled her dark hair back into a messy ponytail, not even bothering to brush it, and she doubted any of the make-up she'd sparingly applied that morning was still clinging to her face but it was too late to worry about her looks now. Thankfully her friends and colleagues were unlikely to be done up to the nines. Anything smarter than hospital scrubs was deemed to be making an effort.

There were plenty of familiar faces in the pub and Kitty said hello to several people as she made her way through the room without pausing to chat for too long. There was one face in particular she was looking for and she didn't want to waste time on other conversations. She wasn't in a particularly sociable mood.

She skimmed over the DJ and looked past him out onto the deck that stretched into the harbour. The Manly ferry was docking at the quay, its lighted windows bright against the twilight sky, and silhouetted against the darkening sky was the person she was looking for.

Joe Harkness.

His broad-shouldered, six-foot frame stood a head above the bevy of women who surrounded him—no surprises there. His short, brown hair was expertly groomed to give him the *I just stepped out of the shower* look and he was laughing at someone's comment. His blue eyes flashed as he laughed and the dimple in his chin only added to his appeal as the women eyed him adoringly. He had a beer in one hand and his other arm slung around the shoulders of one of the women. Again, no surprise. Her life may be a bit of a mess but she could always rely on Joe to be consistent. Happy, charming and gorgeous, he had a constant stream of women moving in and out of his life, there was never a shortage, and Kitty was grateful that he always seemed to have time for her. She didn't want to be one of a string of girlfriends, she wanted to be just what she was—his closest friend.

They'd been friends for almost ten years since meeting on their first day at nursing college. Kitty had been straight out of high school, Joe a couple of years older, having taken a gap year or two before starting university. They'd finished nursing together but had ultimately ended up going in different directions career-wise. She worked in the emergency department at the North Sydney Hospital and Joe had continued his studies and was now an intensive care paramedic. He was based at the ambulance station attached to the hospital, but even if they hadn't ended up in such close proximity Kitty knew they would still have remained friends. In her opinion, everyone needed a Joe in their life.

Someone dependable and loyal. He understood her and he never judged her.

Kitty checked out the unfamiliar woman who was under Joe's arm and wondered who she was. A new girlfriend or just a friend? She hoped it was a new girlfriend. She didn't want Joe to have other female friends. Girlfriends never stayed in his life for long and she was happy to tolerate them. She didn't need to worry about them taking her position as his favourite. She knew he was in no hurry to settle down. He'd told her as much often enough, and she selfishly hoped he meant it. His parents had hardly instilled faith in him about the joys of matrimony or the sanctity of marriage and that pleased Kitty. She didn't want to share him, and she worried that a serious relationship might mean he wouldn't have room for her in his life any more. She needed him and she couldn't imagine not having him in her life.

Joe spotted her as she made her way towards him and he smiled and removed his arm from the woman's shoulders as he stepped forward to greet Kitty. Seeing him so casually separate himself from the woman gave her a tiny ping of satisfaction. New girlfriend or not, she was still more important.

'Hey, what are you doing here?' His smile brought out the dimple in his chin even further and his blue eyes sparkled. 'I thought you said you couldn't make it,' he said as he looked over her shoulder. She knew who he was looking for even as he asked, 'Where's Mike?'

'Out.'

'What's going on?'

Kitty heard the concern in his voice and that was enough to get the tears to well up in her dark brown eyes but she wasn't going to explain her circumstances in front of a complete stranger. She shuffled from foot to foot as Joe excused himself from the women around him. He looped his arm over Kitty's shoulder. 'Come on. It looks like you could use a drink.' He shepherded her across the room as he continued to talk, giving her time and space to get her own thoughts together. 'Does Mike know you're here?'

'No.' She shook her head as she replied and dislodged two fat tears that spilled from her eyes and rolled down her cheeks. She wiped them away with the back of her hand but she wasn't fast enough to stop Joe from noticing.

'What happened? He didn't hit you, did he?' Joe was looking at her carefully. She knew she looked like a mess. Her hair was dishevelled, her eyes red-rimmed and her face was pale. She looked like a woman who'd fled without bothering to brush her hair or grab anything but her handbag.

'No! It's nothing like that.' She was appalled that he might think she'd be in an abusive relationship. She knew he'd seen plenty of domestic violence cases in his role as a paramedic. She'd seen more than her fair share presenting to Emergency as well—too many—and they'd convinced her that she would never stay in a physically abusive relationship.

But what about an emotionally abusive one? After the initial honeymoon period in her relationship with Mike she was beginning to wonder if things were changing. And not for the better.

'We had an argument.' She had to admit that was what it was.

'Well, I'm sure it won't be the last one.'

'I think it could be,' she admitted. 'I think

we might be over.' It was a scary thought. Kitty didn't like being on her own. In fact, she dreaded it and she knew her fear of being alone often caused her to persevere with relationships for longer than she should, but this disagreement with Mike was likely to be the beginning of the end of their relationship. She knew she couldn't stay with him unless he changed his mind.

Early on in their relationship she'd loved the fact that he'd wanted to be her everything. She'd been adrift, lonely, she'd wanted someone to lean on, to make decisions for her, someone who wanted to be all she needed, but did he only want to love her on his terms? Did he even love her? He must know how big a decision this was for her, how she needed his support. If he really was going to push her on this issue then maybe it was time she stood her ground. Staying with him just because it was better than being alone wasn't a good enough reason any more. Not when there could be so much at stake. If she didn't offer to be a surrogate now, Jess and Cam might never get the baby they wanted.

Kitty wanted to be loved but on her terms. She needed to move on from this relationship. She was stronger now. She could be on her own.

She could do this.

She wanted to do this.

And if this worked out she wouldn't be alone. She'd be pregnant. You couldn't be less alone when you were physically attached to another human. A baby would fill all the empty, lonely spots in her heart, satisfy her need to be loved and to have someone to love in return. A baby could be the answer to so many prayers and the solution to so many problems.

A baby was just what her family needed.

Joe struggled to keep the smile off his face as he guided Kitty to one end of the bar where the crowd was marginally thinner. Even though he'd never pretended to like the guy, he had tolerated Mike for Kitty's sake, but he wasn't going to pretend that he'd be unhappy to see him gone from her life.

He held up two fingers, indicating his order, and waited for the barman to pour two beers. 'Talk to me,' he said as he handed a drink to Kitty. He couldn't imagine what had brought this about but whatever it was he was grateful.

Kitty took a long sip of her beer. Joe could see her hand shaking. He'd seen her agitated, upset and emotionally fragile before, but lately she'd seemed to be getting back on top of things. Her life, while certainly not without its dramas and tragedies in the past, had been on a fairly even keel for the past few months and he'd thought she was doing well.

'Jess and Cam want to have a baby,' Kitty said.

'Is that possible?' he asked. A couple of years ago Kitty's sister had been diagnosed with uterine cancer and Joe knew she'd undergone chemotherapy, and he thought the surgeon had performed a total hysterectomy.

'Not in the traditional sense,' Kitty confirmed, 'but Jess froze her eggs before her treatment and now they want to have a baby. They need a surrogate.'

'What's that got to do with you and Mike?' He couldn't see how or why this would affect Kitty and Mike's relationship but as Kitty looked up at him he could see the answer in her eyes. 'You?'

Kitty nodded.

'You want to be their surrogate?' The penny dropped. 'And Mike wasn't happy about the idea?'

'He doesn't want me having another man's baby.'

Joe could understand that. If Kitty was his girlfriend, he might even feel the same way. But he wasn't about to side with Mike. He didn't particularly like the guy, and if Mike was prepared to give Kitty up over this issue then he definitely didn't deserve her.

'He doesn't get that it's not my baby. You know how important Jess is to me. She's all I've got. I don't even know if it's possible to do this but if I can do this for them, I will. He can't stop me.'

'Did he try to?'

'He just told me that if I intend to go ahead with this then he's not going to stick around. I think he expects me to choose him but you know I can't.'

'You've left?'

'Not yet,' she replied. 'We both need some time. I still need to talk to Jess, and I'm hoping Mike might change his mind once he's had a chance to think it over, but if he doesn't then I will make my choice.'

Joe couldn't imagine Mike backing down. He was a surgeon and had the ego to go with his profession. Joe didn't think he was madly in love with Kitty and he imagined Mike would see the surrogacy as an assault to his masculinity. He thought Kitty was going to be disappointed if she expected Mike to change his opinion.

'What can I do?' Joe asked. He would do anything for her. Always had. Always would.

'I need a place to stay,' she told him. 'If I stay at Mike's it will give him an opportunity to try to talk me out of this. I need a bit of space while I work out how to handle this, and I can't stay with Jess. If she knew what had happened tonight she'd try and talk me out of my decision as well, and I'm doing this for me as much as for her and Cam. Can I stay at your place? On the couch would be fine, I don't want to cramp your style.'

'Of course.' If all she needed from him was a place to stay while she got things sorted then that's what he would give her. And if it meant Kitty went ahead with the idea and Mike ended the relationship Joe wasn't going to pretend he didn't like the sound of that. 'And just for the record, I think it's a fantastic gesture,' he added. He would be as supportive as possible of this exercise.

'Thank you. I knew you'd understand.'

Her brown eyes were still shiny with tears but at least they weren't spilling over her cheeks any more, although she still looked as if she needed a hug. He opened his arms and she stepped into his embrace. He wrapped his arms around her, closed his eyes briefly and inhaled the familiar vanilla scent of her shampoo as he comforted her.

He hated seeing her upset and he would go to just about any lengths to protect her. He had friends, lots of them, but none of his friendships enjoyed the same closeness that he and Kitty shared. Both of them found something in their relationship that they didn't get from anyone else. That sense of being understood without the need for explanation. He wasn't close to his family and avoided serious romantic relationships, but his relationship with Kitty was proof that he was capable of sustaining a meaningful connection.

It proved to him that he wasn't a complete emotional failure. That he could love someone and maintain a long-term relationship, even if it was platonic. He didn't doubt he wasn't cut out for marriage and commitment. He had no evidence that long-term monogamy was for him. His parents certainly hadn't subscribed to that ideology, they'd had five marriages between them, and Joe himself knew he grew bored and irritated if any of his romantic relationships stretched past a few months.

Some of his friends were convinced that he just hadn't met the perfect girl but Joe wasn't sure she existed. Even perfection had a use-by date in his opinion. From what he'd seen, marriages ended in one of three ways—divorce, death or disinterest—and he didn't see the point. But in the absence of other relationships his connection with Kitty became even more important, and he would do whatever was necessary to maintain it. He intended to always be there for her in a way that others hadn't been.

'But if you're going to do this,' he told her, 'then you need a long-term plan. You need to make some decisions about the next few months, not just about tonight.'

'I know,' she sighed, 'but right now, tonight is all I can manage.'

CHAPTER TWO

'HOLY CRAP!'

Kitty was signing notes at the nurses' station in the emergency department when the ED clerk's exclamation interrupted her concentration. She looked up and saw Lisa's eyes fixed on the wall-mounted television screen.

In the centre of the screen was a burning bus.

Orange flames leapt into the air from the rear and thick black smoke billowed around the vehicle and over several cars that had stopped haphazardly around it. In the background, Kitty could see a sandstone pylon and the heavy iron framework of the Harbour Bridge.

The time was fixed in the bottom right hand corner of the screen. Eight thirty-four a.m. Morning rush hour. This was happening in the middle of her city, a few kilometres from her hospital, and the images were being broadcast live from one of the news helicopters.

Kitty's heart was racing. What was going on? Was it a bomb? In the middle of Sydney?

The volume was muted on the television but Kitty could read the words scrolling across the screen under the picture.

Bus goes up in flames.
Harbour Bridge closed.
Morning traffic disrupted.
Use alternative route.

Traffic had come to a standstill but there was no mention of what had caused the bus to catch fire.

Kitty couldn't tear her eyes from the fiery disaster that was unfolding on the screen in front of her as the helicopter camera zoomed in on the chaos. People were out of their cars, doors left hanging open as they ran. Some ran towards the burning bus, others away. Kitty could see a man with a fire extinguisher aimed futilely at the flames as people stumbled from the bus. He was joined by another half-dozen men, all wearing hi-visibility vests and hard hats, and a couple were carrying additional fire extinguishers, but from what Kitty could see the extra hands were having no impact on the fire.

The live feed widened to show the emergency vehicles, the ambulances and fire engines, their red and blue lights absorbed by the thick cloud of black smoke as they weaved their way through the stationary cars on the bridge.

The images from the helicopter cut out and were replaced by a reporter standing on the bridge, a microphone held up to her mouth and the burning bus behind her. How the hell had she got through the traffic and the chaos? Sitting on the ground around her were several people who looked dazed and shocked. Some were coughing and Kitty wondered if they were passengers from the bus.

Lisa grabbed the remote and pressed a button, increasing the volume until they could hear the reporter's commentary.

'...*on the Harbour Bridge, where a city-bound commuter bus has gone up in flames near the northern end. Witnesses say twenty to thirty passengers have been evacuated but there may still be people trapped inside the bus...'*

Kitty didn't want to see the reporter. She wanted the camera to go back to the accident—she was looking for Joe. But the reporter continued to talk.

'There is no word yet on what caused the fire. Commuters say there was a loud explosion, and you can see behind me that the windows of the bus have all been blown out.'

The camera panned to the bus, zooming in on the accident, and Kitty searched the scene.

'The heat is intense, the sky is thick with black smoke and there is a terrible odour in the air. Paramedics are treating victims for smoke inhalation as firefighters try to get the blaze under control.'

Kitty's eyes flicked from one paramedic to another, from one blue uniform to the next, but she couldn't see Joe. She knew he was working this morning and that crews from the station at the North Sydney Hospital would be some of the closest to the scene. Maybe he was on another call-out? As long as he was safe, she thought—just as she saw a familiar shape at the side of the screen. Smoke was obscuring the image, but she recognised the way he moved.

Joe.

He was running straight at the bus. Her eyes followed his path as he came further into view in the centre of the television screen. There was a man standing in the doorway of the bus, his back to Joe. He was bent over, and he looked like he was struggling with something. Kitty realised he was dragging someone from the bus. And then Joe was there, followed by two other paramedics.

The standing man stepped out of the way as the paramedics threw a blanket over the man who lay in the doorway before lifting him from the bus and putting him on a stretcher.

Kitty could see the other man swaying as he stood next to the bus. Just when he looked as if he was about to collapse Joe caught him and laid him on the ground.

The camera panned out again and the reporter was in the foreground of the shot, blocking Kitty's view. She could see the man lying on the ground but she couldn't see Joe. He wouldn't have gone *into* the bus, would he? Surely not? That would be the firefighters' job. But was he far enough away? What if there was another explosion?

'Firefighters are struggling to douse the flames engulfing a city-bound bus on the Harbour Bridge,' the reporter repeated. *'All lanes on the bridge are closed until the danger is contained. It appears that the bus has now been evacuated with reports that two men, the driver and a passenger, are being treated for burns, but there are no reports of any fatalities at this stage and still no information as to the cause of the fire.'*

There was an increase in activity in the background and finally the camera cut away from the reporter and back to the bus. Kitty could see ambulances, their doors open and lights flashing as the picture showed someone being loaded in through the back doors of one of them.

And there was Joe. Back in view. She couldn't see his face but she didn't need to. He was instantly recognisable. It was more than the width of his shoulders and the shape of his head. It was the way he moved. Purposeful, composed. Unflappable, measured. Despite the chaos of his surroundings he projected calmness. He always seemed to know what he was doing. Not like her. So often she felt completely lost unless he was there to anchor her. Joe had been there for her in the toughest of times, but he'd never seemed to need her in the same way.

He was leaning over one of the victims, but he looked awfully close to the burning bus. Too close. Kitty's heart was still racing. She was trapped in a terrible feeling of helplessness. What if something happened to him?

She tried to push that thought aside as she saw him loading his patient onto the stretcher. She couldn't bear to think of something happening to Joe. He was a constant, solid, reassuring presence, the calm through so many of her storms, and she couldn't imagine her life without him in it. She turned away from the television as Joe disappeared from the screen, willing him to hurry before anything else could go wrong.

He would be on his way to her now. She knew he would be coming to her hospital. She needed to see him, to reassure herself he was OK.

Lisa muted the television as Kitty brought her focus back to the task at hand. The ambulances would be arriving soon. They needed to be ready. The paramedics would be turning around and bringing the injured to the North Sydney Hospital. They might not be the closest but they were on the right side of the bridge, on the same side of the harbour. They would be the most easily accessible emergency department, and they had a burns unit. Time was of the essence, especially for burns victims.

Kitty grabbed aprons and left Lisa to deal with the patients waiting for attention. She would have to explain to them that there was a bigger emergency that had to be dealt with before they could be seen.

Davina, the charge nurse, was assembling her troops and assigning them to teams. Kitty saw Mike arrive, tying his apron over his scrubs. She hadn't seen him since she'd walked out three days ago. Hadn't worked with him, hadn't taken his calls. She'd replied to his messages but that had been all she'd been capable of. She hadn't felt ready for another discussion that would more than likely end in another argument. She needed to have her argument prepared.

She breathed a sigh of relief when she wasn't assigned to Mike's team. She had no idea if that had been deliberate on Davina's part, she didn't think anyone knew about what was going on, but she was grateful. She needed to focus and she didn't need the distraction of worrying about what Mike may or may not be thinking.

'The information I've got is that we have two burns victims coming in. Priority One. Mike, you take the first one, his injuries are more extensive and you've got the most experience. Anna,' she said, nodding at the other doctor, 'your team can take the other. We'll triage any other patients on arrival,' Davina finished as the first ambulance pulled in to the emergency bay.

Kitty pulled on a pair of disposable gloves and craned her neck as the ambulance doors opened, trying to see which paramedics were in attendance.

She couldn't see Joe.

'Young adult male. Unresponsive. Burns to his legs and arms.' She heard the information being disseminated as the patient was wheeled past her but she was already turning away, turning back to the road, on the lookout for the next ambulance.

She waited nervously, hoping the next unit

would bring Joe. When her parents had been killed in a car accident, and again when Jess had been diagnosed with cancer and throughout her treatment, Kitty had always been able to rely on him and she couldn't imagine how she would cope if anything happened to him.

She shook her head, clearing her mind as another ambulance pulled in. Anna had her hand on the rear door and she swung it open. Kitty exhaled as Joe emerged from the back. Broad shoulders, long legs, spiky hair. Strong and solid. He reached for the stretcher, pulling it from the ambulance. He bent his head and she could see him talking to his patient. His voice would be calm, reassuring.

Kitty stepped closer as Joe's partner slammed the driver's door and came to help manoeuvre the stretcher.

Joe was filthy. His uniform was covered in black soot and Kitty could smell smoke, diesel fuel and burning rubber. The smell seemed to have permeated the clothes of the paramedics and the victim, but at least Joe appeared to be in one piece.

'Hey! I thought I might find you here,' he said as she fell into step alongside him.

'You're OK?' she asked. When he nodded

she glanced over his shoulder. 'How many more are there?'

'Only two seriously injured. The rest are smoke inhalation victims and assorted, non-life-threatening orthopaedic injuries.'

Kitty knew it could have been worse. Joe didn't say anything in front of their patient but Kitty could hear in his voice and she'd seen the scene for herself. Two burns victims, no fatalities and some people suffering from smoke inhalation and a few fractures was a pretty good outcome. It could have been *much* worse. But their patient didn't need to hear that.

'This is Carlos, the bus driver, fifty-three years old, second-degree burns to his hands and arms. Smoke inhalation but airway not compromised.'

Kitty looked down at Carlos. He had a sheet pulled halfway up his chest covering his arms but she could see an ID badge on his shirt pocket and she could just make out the bus company logo. His shirt, like Joe's, was blackened with soot, and he had an oxygen mask covering his nose and mouth but Kitty took that to be a precautionary measure given Joe's summary.

As they pushed the stretcher through the hospital doors and into an exam room, Joe drew back the sheet that had been tented over Carlos's forearms in an attempt to protect him from exposure to bacteria. His hands were bright pink, the skin blistered and hairless, and the burns extended halfway up his forearms. Someone had inserted an IV cannula into his elbow but no fluids had been connected. His transfer had been less than thirty minutes so there had been no urgency.

Kitty grabbed a slide board and prepared to transfer Carlos from the stretcher. She stood next to Joe and waited while Anna and the other paramedic carefully rolled Carlos. She and Joe slid the board under their patient.

'On three.' The transfer went smoothly and Joe and his partner stepped out of the way, removing their stretcher and leaving Kitty and Anna to get to work. With a wink in her direction, Joe was gone.

Kitty didn't waste time. Anna was cutting Carlos's shirt away as Kitty replaced his oxygen mask and attached monitors. She and Anna worked together well. She was an experienced ED doctor and Kitty liked working with her. She was methodical and didn't miss much.

'Carlos, I'm Dr Lewis. Kitty and I will look after you. Do you have any medical issues we need to be aware of? Any heart problems, diabetes? Anything like that?'

Carlos shook his head.

'I'm just going to take your oxygen mask off to check your airway,' Anna explained softly.

Kitty recorded Carlos's heart rate, blood pressure and respiration rate while Anna did her examination. She replaced the oxygen mask with tubing once Anna was finished, looping it over his ears and sliding the pegs into his nose. She recorded his oxygen levels as Anna kept talking.

'We need to replace your lost fluid and get these burns cleaned up. I'm going to give you something for the pain, OK?'

They worked quickly through their initial assessment, needing to get a handle on the extent of Carlos's injuries. Some, like his burned skin, were obvious but damage to his lungs was less easy to spot and more likely to cause problems, although often not for a day or two. They had to prioritise.

Anna attached a bag of saline to the cannula in Carlos's elbow to replace the fluids he'd lost while Kitty distracted him, asking questions about his family. 'Is there anyone you want us to call?'

'The paramedics called my wife. Someone is bringing her to the hospital, but can you tell me how the boy is?' His voice was raspy and breathless. It sounded painful to talk and Kitty was sure she'd heard correctly. Boy?

She frowned. Was Carlos delirious? Her gaze flicked to the monitors. His temperature was raised but not excessively. 'What boy?'

'The one I pulled from the bus. Did he make it?'

Kitty realised he was talking about the other victim. Their first patient. 'You pulled him out?' The vision she'd watched on the television flashed back in her mind. The man dragging the other body from the bus. The standing man. The one who'd looked as if he'd been about to collapse only Joe had caught him just in time. That had been Carlos. 'Is that when you got burnt?'

Carlos nodded and struggled to talk. To explain. 'When the fire started it was just a bit of smoke. I stopped and told everyone to get off but the boy only got as far as me and said something about his bag. He ran back down the aisle before I could stop him. Then something exploded. The windows of the bus blew out and he got caught in the flames. I couldn't leave him.'

Kitty glanced at Anna, communicating mutely. Carlos would be hailed a hero, which meant the hospital would be swarming with media. They would all want a piece of him.

In silent consultation they agreed to take their time treating him, giving him a chance to catch his breath, and then they'd see if he wanted to make a statement. There were lots of variables and it wasn't Kitty's place to comment on what he should do.

'He was in a bad way. Do you know how he is?' Carlos asked, oblivious to the silent exchange going on between Kitty and Anna. He appeared to be more concerned about the boy than himself.

'He's here,' Kitty told him. 'He was brought in just before you. He's being looked after.'

'So he's alive?'

'As far as I know,' she said. She didn't know what else she could tell Carlos. She didn't have any more information and she wouldn't be able to disclose anything she did know. She was sure that if the boy survived he'd want to thank Carlos personally. She hoped so.

Anna and Kitty worked slowly and meticulously. They washed the burnt skin on Carlos's arms and hands and debrided the blisters, applying antibiotic cream before carefully separating his fingers and wrapping them individually.

'Will your wife be able to manage at home with you?' Kitty asked as she finished wrapping the last finger. 'We will need to keep you here for a few hours, just to keep an eye on you, but then if your readings are all within normal limits you'll be able to go home. You'll need to have some follow-up appointments for your lungs, though, and we will also make you an appointment with the burns unit in a few days. It's here in the hospital. Will someone be able to drive you here?'

'My wife doesn't drive.'

'That's OK,' Kitty replied. 'I'll speak to your employer. They will have to arrange transport for you seeing as this was a workplace accident. Is that OK with you?'

Carlos nodded.

'All right, let's get you comfortable and then I'll pop out and see if your wife is here yet.'

Kitty ducked into the staff kitchen for a break while Carlos had a few minutes with his wife. As all the other accident victims were being taken care of she decided she'd take the chance to top up her caffeine level. As she'd expected, the waiting room was now crowded with reporters all wanting to get an interview with Carlos, but she'd leave that decision to him. She skirted the waiting room and was just adding sugar to her coffee when Mike walked in.

He looked tired and Kitty was worried that things hadn't gone smoothly. He had been treating the boy from the bus, the one Carlos had saved. Kitty hoped it hadn't been in vain. She forgot that she'd barely spoken to him since their argument. At work things were different. She could put her personal issues aside. She'd learnt to compartmentalise her life and, in fact, the hospital often provided an escape. For the most part, no matter how bad things were in her own life, work was a constant reminder that she wasn't the only one suffering. On a couple of occasions she had felt that her life sucked more than her patients', but she always found work to be a good distraction. Right now, her disagreement with Mike was minor compared to their day so far. Things weren't so bad that she couldn't reach out to him.

'How did it go?'

'He's alive but he has burns to about thirty per cent of his body and to his airway. He's been transferred to the burns unit.' He ran his hands through his hair. 'All because he left his laptop behind.' He shook his head. It sounded ridiculous but Kitty guessed the boy hadn't stopped to think about the consequences. Hadn't thought about the risks. And now it was too late. What's done was done. She knew better than most that there was no going back. The past couldn't be changed no matter how much you might wish it.

Mike filled a glass from the water cooler. 'When are you coming home?' he asked over his shoulder.

'That depends,' she said, knowing she wasn't telling the truth. She didn't think she would be going back. 'Have you changed your mind about my plans?'

'No.'

Which meant he assumed she'd changed *her* mind.

'Well, I haven't either,' she said.

His voice was quiet, his tone not malicious, but he sounded very definite as he said, 'I'm not going to be a cuckold in my own house.'

That was part of the problem. Even though she'd moved in with him after six months and had now been living with him for five, it was still his house. Not theirs. He still held all the cards, still had all the control.

'It's hardly the same thing,' she argued.

'It is to me,' he said as he drained his glass. 'You will be pregnant with another man's baby.'

'But surely you can understand my reasons?'

He was shaking his head. 'I can't imagine what could possibly make you want to do this. Jess has other options.'

'But she's my sister!' That was another part of the problem. He really didn't get her need for family. He didn't get her desperate desire to hold onto what was left of it.

'IVF isn't an option,' Kitty said, even though Mike knew that. Jess had been diagnosed with uterine cancer three years ago and after harvesting and storing her eggs she'd had a total hysterectomy, meaning that the simplest option was not an option. 'That leaves adoption or surrogacy. They're not likely to be approved for adoption given Jess's medical history, and finding someone else to offer to be a surrogate could take months—years even.'

Surrogacy in Australia was heavily legislated. Each state had its own laws and although New South Wales was a bit more lenient than other parts of the country, surrogate mothers couldn't be paid. They could be reimbursed for their medical costs but couldn't benefit financially, which meant that would-be parents needed to find someone who would do it out of the kindness of their hearts. It wasn't like asking someone to mind your pets while you went on a holiday—you were asking someone to lend you their body for forty weeks or more. Asking someone to subject themselves to tests and procedures to fulfil your own dreams. It wasn't easy.

Kitty closed her eyes and pictured Jess holding a baby. Her baby.

She opened her eyes and looked at Mike.

Those was her choices. Mike or her sister's baby.

'You can't be their only solution,' he said.

'Maybe not,' she replied. 'But I am their best one.'

Mike's pager beeped and he pulled it from his waistband to read the message. He glanced up and Kitty knew he was about to leave, but she also knew he'd want the last word. True to form he said, 'If you want to do this you'll have to do it without any help from me.'

He didn't wait for a reply before he turned and left the room.

Kitty stood still for a moment, trying to figure out what had just happened. She thought about what she was doing. What she was giving up. Why was her sister's happiness more important than her own?

Jess's happiness would be shared by Kitty. If she could give her sister an opportunity to have a family then, by association, she would benefit too—she'd be giving herself more family. She did want a family of her own one day but she knew Mike wasn't the man she would do that with. She had to believe her time would come, and meanwhile she'd do what she could. So she would grant Jess's wish. That would bring her happiness too. Being a surrogate meant giving up Mike but it was a sacrifice Kitty was willing to make.

She was still standing in the centre of the room when Joe walked in.

'Is everything OK?' he asked. He'd changed into a clean uniform and washed his face. He looked good in his uniform. The blue suited him, brought out the colour of his eyes, but it was more than that. It was the air of responsibility it gave him. He wore it well. He looked strong, capable and dependable. All the things she knew him to be were accentuated by the uniform. 'Rough day?'

She shook her head. 'No worse than usual. I was just thinking...'

Joe grinned. 'Should I be worried?'

She laughed. She hadn't realised she'd felt like laughing but Joe could always lift her spirits. 'Maybe,' she replied.

'What's going on?'

'You just missed Mike.'

'And?' He hesitated before asking, 'You're not thinking of moving back in?'

Kitty shook her head. 'No. But we had another discussion about the surrogacy. I wasn't prepared for it and I know I didn't handle it all that well, but he's still making it all about him.' Like always, she nearly added but she stopped herself, realising that was unfair. At work Mike was single-minded, putting his patients' needs first. He was focussed and dedicated—maybe all that effort at work made him think he deserved to be at the top of his own list of priorities away from work too, but sometimes she wished she felt as important to him as he felt to himself. 'This isn't about him,' she continued. 'It's not even about me. It's about Jess and Cam. Why can't he see that?'

Joe raised an eyebrow. 'You really want to hear my answer to that question?'

'No, I guess not.' Kitty managed a half-smile. 'But I'm tired of feeling like my opinions don't matter.'

'So what next?'

'I need to talk to Jess and Cam.'

'You're doing this?'

'I am.' She smiled. She'd made a decision and it felt good. She knew it was the right one. She hated being alone but she was willing to sacrifice her relationship with Mike in order to give her sister a baby. Family was more important to her than anything. She'd lost so many members of her family already. First her baby sister had died when Kitty had been just five years old and then, fourteen years later, both her parents had gone too. To offer Jess and Cam the baby they longed for would help to compensate for everything and everyone they'd already lost. 'Provided Jess and Cam agree.'

'I can't imagine they won't.'

'No.' Her smile widened. 'It's perfect. My family needs something good to look forward to, something positive, after everything that has happened.' She needed it too. 'I'll go and see them after work today and then I need to find a new place to live.'

'You know you're welcome to stay with me for as long as you need to.'

'Thanks, but I can't put you out of your bed.' Joe had already spent the past couple of nights on his couch, giving up his bed for Kitty, but that wasn't a long-term solution. 'You said yourself I needed a more permanent plan. I'll figure something out.'

CHAPTER THREE

KITTY STACKED THE empty dinner plates and took them into the kitchen. She had invited herself to Jess and Cam's for dinner and had promised to do the dishes in return, but she wanted to have the discussion she had planned first. Her ultimate agenda was to raise her surrogacy suggestion.

'A little while ago you mentioned that you were thinking about investigating the option of surrogacy using your frozen embryos,' she said to them both as she returned to the table. 'Have you done anything about that?'

'Not officially,' Cam replied. 'We've done some research but it's not a straightforward exercise. We think we'd like to find someone privately who's willing to act as a surrogate but we're not sure how to go about that. If we can't find someone privately we'll have to advertise and that's tricky here, but we can't afford to go overseas to do it. It's not going to be easy.'

'But we have to try,' Jess added.

'I know it's not easy,' Kitty said, looking into her sister's dark eyes. A mirror of her own face looked back at her. There was no mistaking they were sisters. They had the same dark eyes and dark hair, although Jess's was shorter and had grown back with a slight wave in it after the chemotherapy. Jess's face was more oval than Kitty's, whose own face could only be described as round. It made Kitty look young for her years but she was old enough to know what she was doing. She took a deep breath and held Jess's gaze. 'I would like to do it for you.'

'What?'

'I want to be your surrogate.'

'Really?'

'Really.'

'You're serious?'

Kitty nodded and Jess broke into a wide smile. She really was pretty when she smiled, Kitty thought as her sister bounced out of her chair and threw her arms around her. 'I can't believe this! Thank you!'

'Why?' Cam asked.

Cam's reaction took Kitty by surprise. To be honest, she'd thought they'd both be ecstatic but while Jess was obviously delighted and grateful, Cameron was far more reserved.

'That doesn't matter, Cam,' Jess remonstrated. 'All that matters is that Kitty is offering.' Jess was crying now as she continued to hug Kitty. Tears were running down her cheeks and soaking into Kitty's shirt. Kitty was pretty sure they were happy tears.

'I'm not saying I don't appreciate your offer,' Cam said as Jess finally let go of her little sister. 'It's very generous, but it's not as simple as you might think. I expect we'll all have questions, and one of mine is: why?'

In contrast, Jess didn't appear to have any questions. Kitty knew she was far too emotional and too caught up in the idea that she could become a mum to worry about the intricacies and details, but Cam deserved answers.

'You and Jess are my only family,' Kitty explained. 'You're all I've got. If I can give you the baby that Jess desperately wants I get to expand my family. It's a win-win situation.'

'But you can have your own children,' Cam argued. 'You're twenty-seven, this might take up the next two years of your life. Even if this works straight away it's not like you can be pregnant tomorrow. There are meetings, counselling, legalities to sort through. Trust me, we know what's involved, we've looked at everything. It's not straightforward and it will take time. What if you want to have your own baby in the meantime?'

'I'm not at the stage where I want to have a baby.'

'But that might change at any point in the next year or two. And what about Mike? He's older than you, what if he wants children sooner?'

Kitty shook her head. 'I don't think he wants that.' It didn't matter what he wanted, she wasn't going to have babies with Mike anyway. She knew now more than ever that she didn't want him to be the father of her children. He was too intense. Too controlling. She wanted someone fun. She *needed* someone fun. She needed someone to inject that into her life as well as her children's. She knew she had a tendency to get a bit low and she needed laughter and light in her life. That's why she loved being around Joe.

She didn't mention that she'd broken up with Mike. If Jess thought it was because of her decision to offer to be their surrogate Kitty knew she might decline her offer, and she was desperate to do this. Desperate to give Jess the baby she wanted. That bit of news could wait for another day.

'I want to do this.' Kitty would put her life on hold indefinitely in order to give Jess the baby she wanted—the baby Kitty thought they all needed. 'Can't we at least investigate the idea?'

'Yes.' Jess was quick to agree and Kitty knew then that her offer had been accepted. She knew Cam didn't have the heart to refuse his wife. Kitty knew he would give Jess anything she asked for if it were possible, and this just might be possible. At least they would get to try.

Kitty picked up the pen and signed on the dotted line next to Cam and Jess's signatures. The lawyer witnessed their scrawls and stamped the pages. Signing the surrogacy agreement that had been drawn up was almost the final step in the process. Next their application would be reviewed by the IVF ethics committee and, if approved, she would become a surrogate. Not if, she told herself—

when. She had to think positively. There was
no reason not to think this wouldn't go ahead.

Over the past two months she had been
poked and prodded, examined and tested, but
she didn't mind. The tests hadn't raised any
red flags and she was told she was a good
candidate. She knew the clinic would have
preferred it if she had borne children already
as it left less room for surprises or problems
with the pregnancy and delivery, but it wasn't
a requirement in New South Wales, as it was
in some other parts of the country, and for that
Kitty was grateful. And the tests had given
no indication that she wouldn't have a normal
pregnancy. She was a healthy twenty-seven-
year-old. She was convinced there wouldn't
be any problems and fortunately that seemed
to be the conclusion after all the tests were
completed.

As a single woman in Sydney Kitty could
access the medical care she needed as a surrogate. Jess and Cam had agreed to pay any
out-of-pocket expenses, which could be quite
costly, but they had no complaints. All three
of them had attended a medical review at Jess
and Cam's fertility clinic and they had all undergone the mandatory counselling sessions,

though fortunately they hadn't been sent for independent psychiatric reviews. The lawyer had briefed them on their rights and obligations and had drawn up the agreement, and now they had one last hurdle. Kitty crossed her fingers that the ethics committee would approve their request.

'Kitty Nelson?'

She looked up as the fertility nurse called her name. This was it.

She was going to be a surrogate. The ethics committee had approved their application and now, if everything went according to plan, in nine months' time she would deliver a healthy baby for Jess and Cam, and her, to love.

Jess's eggs had been fertilised and the embryos created. All that was left was the implantation.

Kitty stood up and Jess followed suit. Kitty was surprised to find her legs were shaky. There was a lot of expectation riding on today but she hadn't realised she had felt the pressure. There wasn't much about it she could control, but now that the moment had come she desperately hoped she would turn out to be the perfect host. The perfect surrogate for a perfect baby.

'Are you sure you don't want me to come in with you?' Jess asked.

Kitty could hear the pleading note in her voice but she'd made up her mind and she was going to stand firm on this point.

She reached over and held Jess's hand.

'I don't watch you and Cam making babies, I'm not going to let you watch me getting impregnated.'

Cam was by the window, looking out at the city streets several floors below, pacing up and down, already looking like an expectant father. Fortunately *he* hadn't asked to watch.

'Cam and I didn't make this baby the traditional way.'

'I know, but it would still be weird to have you in the room.'

'But you're happy for us to be there when the baby is born?'

Kitty nodded. 'Of course!' Although she'd have some ground rules then too—for instance, Cam would have to stay away from the business end, but she would discuss that later. Her first priority was to get pregnant.

'OK,' Jess said as she wrapped Kitty in a hug. 'Good luck.'

Kitty could feel Jess's bones as she hugged her sister back. She was still way too thin. 'It'll be fine.'

'I can't believe that in a matter of minutes you could be pregnant. I'm going to be a mum.'

If everything went to plan, Kitty thought, but she kept quiet. She needed to be in a positive frame of mind. She needed to believe this was going to work. A new life, a new member of the family to love, was just what they all needed. After their baby sister had drowned at the age of two, and then losing their parents in a car accident when Kitty was just nineteen, followed by Jess's shock cancer diagnosis two and a half years ago, they needed something to look forward to.

She kissed Jess's cheek and stepped back. 'See you soon.'

Joe was watching the clock, hoping he didn't get a last-minute call-out before the end of his night shift. It had been busy, but that wasn't uncommon. Saturday nights were always frantic, filled with the usual jobs—drunk and

disorderly men getting into fights, drug over-
doses, car accidents, car versus pedestrian accidents, heart attacks or indigestion that people
mistook for heart attacks... The new crew was
due at any moment and if the phones remained
quiet for five more minutes he'd get out of
there on time. He kept his fingers crossed. If
he got out on time he might catch Kitty.

He was missing her company. The week
that she'd stayed with him was now months
ago but he'd got used to having her around
and the months since she'd been gone had
dragged. But at least she wasn't back with
Mike. She'd moved out of Joe's apartment
and in with Jess and Cam. They'd decided
that it would be the best place for Kitty to
live while they went through the surrogacy
application and hopefully a successful pregnancy. That way Jess figured she'd get to be
involved every step of the way. They'd assumed that the surrogacy process would be
successful. Joe could understand why—what
was the point of going ahead with the plan if
you thought it was going to fail? But he was
worried that they could all be setting themselves up for heartache.

Kitty had had enough heartache in her life.

But he'd barely seen her since she'd moved out. She'd been caught up in the surrogacy plans and even at work their paths hadn't crossed often. Although he was based at the ambulance station adjacent to the North Sydney Hospital, even their shifts hadn't coincided much, and more often than not when he'd brought patients to the ED or called in on a break she hadn't been rostered on.

His shift finished on time and he was able to get across to the ED before Kitty left the hospital. He sighed in relief.

'Hi.' He greeted her as she walked through the exit.

'Joe!' Her smile lit up her face and he found himself beaming back at her. It was good to see her. Really good. 'Have you finished your shift?' she asked.

'Yep. Signed out, all done.'

'Well, your timing is perfect,' she said as she tucked her hand through his elbow and fell into step beside him. 'I need to talk to you and I'm starving. Have you got time for breakfast?'

'Sure.'

They walked the few blocks to their regular café on Manly Beach and grabbed a table with a view over the water. The sun was still low in the sky but after a night cooped up in the hospital Joe knew that Kitty would want to be outside despite the glare.

Joe ordered his usual big breakfast while Kitty chose fresh fruit, yoghurt and muesli. She was restless, her feet jiggled constantly, and she was sitting on the edge of her seat. 'Are you going to be able to sit still long enough to eat?' he asked.

'Not unless I tell you my news first.'

'Go on, then,' Joe said as the waitress brought a coffee for him and a green tea for Kitty.

'I did a pregnancy test yesterday.'

'Already?'

Kitty nodded. 'It's two weeks tomorrow since the procedure.'

He knew that. He'd been keeping tabs on the process. He didn't need to ask what the result was, he could see in her eyes—excitement was written all over her face. He didn't need her to tell him the result but she told him anyway.

'It was positive!'

'You know it could be a false positive this early.' He didn't *think* he wanted to burst her bubble of happiness but his comment was out before he'd had time to censor it. He'd done some research and he knew the fertility clinics advised their patients not to do home tests but to wait for the official blood test. He assumed it was because there were too many occasions when people got false positive results.

'I know.' Kitty nodded. 'But I couldn't resist. I *feel* like it's worked. My boobs are tender…' She pressed on her boobs and Joe had to force himself to avert his eyes. He didn't want to be caught looking. 'And I *had* to know.'

'Who else have you told?'

Kitty frowned, a little crease appearing between her dark brows. 'No one. The official blood test is still a couple of days away so I won't say anything to Jess until then, but I had to tell someone. I wanted to tell you.'

Joe knew he should be pleased, he knew how much this meant to her. He appreciated that she'd shared her news with him but he was surprised to find he was experiencing another unexpected emotion. He could taste it.

The sour taste of jealousy.

He had never actually considered what

would happen when Kitty eventually settled down and had babies. He knew it was what she wanted but he hadn't thought about the ramifications, the reality. He hadn't thought about the fact that she would have other priorities in her life, that there would be someone more important than him.

It hurt to realise she was going to have this experience without him. To realise he wasn't going to be part of this experience except in the role of a bystander. This baby wouldn't be hers to keep—but seeing her so excited about it reminded him that eventually that *would* happen and what would that mean for them?

For him?

He pushed down the sense of jealousy—now was not the time or the place to give in to his own emotions—and raised his coffee in a toast, hoping that somehow he would manage to say the right thing.

'Congratulations,' he said as he forced a smile.

Kitty fidgeted in her seat as she forced herself to eat her lunch as she sat across from Cam and Jess. She was on tenterhooks and had been for the past few days, ever since she'd taken the home pregnancy test. She'd thought that by sharing her news with Joe it would settle her excitement to a point where it would be bearable but she still couldn't wait for Jess and Cam to hear the results. It was all anyone wanted.

She was positive the procedure had worked but she hadn't said anything as she really didn't want to get Jess's hopes up. Now, after having to wait for the official test, she started having doubts. What if it hadn't worked? What if the home pregnancy test she'd done *had* given her a false positive? What if all the symptoms she'd been experiencing were just the result of her over-active imagination or wishful thinking? Surely life wouldn't be so cruel?

She placed her elbows on the table as the waitress cleared the remains of their lunch away. She leant forward and her breasts squashed against her forearms. Her boobs were definitely still tender, that had to mean something. She knew false positives were unlikely in those home testing kits. False negatives were far more common—and, besides, she'd also gone off coffee. She'd cut down on her caffeine before the embryonic transfer at the same time as she'd started taking folic acid tablets—she'd wanted to do everything she could to ensure that this worked—but now she couldn't even stand the *taste* of coffee. Something that had been one of her favourite drinks now tasted bitter, making it easy to stay off it.

Her fingers fidgeted and played with the gauze bandage that was wrapped around her left elbow, a constant reminder of what she was waiting for. She'd had the official blood test and she and Jess and Cam were just killing time until they could return to the IVF clinic to hear the results. Kitty was desperate to get back there.

Finally, with ten minutes before they were due back, Cam paid for their meals and they headed for the door.

'All right,' the doctor said as they were ushered into the consulting room and took their seats. 'We were testing for hCG in the blood. Any increase in hCG levels in a surrogate indicates a positive pregnancy but the levels are significant. The higher the better. Higher levels suggest a viable pregnancy. At this point in time, two weeks post-implantation, we expect to see levels above fifty milli-international units per millilitre.' Kitty wished she'd just get on with it. The wait was agonising. 'But we're hoping for numbers closer to five hundred.' There was a sheet of paper sitting on the desk. The doctor glanced down at it and when she looked up she was smiling. 'Your numbers are four hundred and fifty. Congratulations, you are pregnant.'

'Oh, my God, you did it.' Jess jumped up from her chair and hugged Kitty. 'Thank you so much. I can't believe it.' Tears were running down her cheeks as she turned to Cam. 'We're going to have a baby!' she said as she threw her arms around him.

Cam was grinning from ear to ear as he hugged and then kissed his wife before hugging Kitty. Jess was bawling and Kitty could feel her own tears threatening to spill from her eyes. She'd been positive that the embryo transfer had been successful but she hadn't dared to believe it and the relief was almost as great as the excitement.

The doctor let them celebrate the news and when they all managed to get their emotions under control she continued the consult. 'Before I let you go I'll just run through the next steps with you.'

The three of them pulled themselves together long enough to listen to the procedure from here on.

'If everything goes according to plan,' she said, looking at Kitty, 'your hCG levels should double every forty-eight hours. Fast increases in levels are what we are hoping for as that appears to indicate a good pregnancy outcome. I would like to do a follow-up blood test in two days to check those levels. Depending on the results we might then schedule more blood tests but I will also book you in for an ultrasound scan in a fortnight.'

'We'll be able to see our baby that early?' Jess asked.

'Your baby will look like a jelly bean still at that stage but we should be able to see and hear a foetal heartbeat then,' the doctor explained.

Kitty didn't remember much after that, and neither did Jess, she suspected. They were both too excited with the news. They left it to Cam to pay attention to the next round of appointments as they let their minds run wild with the thought of creating a new life. A baby.

* * *

'Kitty, incoming ambulance.'

Kitty was tidying an exam room when Davina stuck her head in and called for her attention. 'We've got a twenty-nine-year-old woman with abdominal pain and the doctors are all busy. Can you meet them in the bay?'

Kitty tucked a clean sheet onto the exam bed and carried the dirty linen out with her, tossing it into a linen bag on her way outside. She exited the doors as the ambulance pulled into the bay and Joe climbed out, pulling the stretcher with him.

'Hey,' he greeted Kitty with his megawatt smile. 'Kitty, this is Talia. Acute abdominal pain. BP one-forty over ninety. Heart rate one hundred and ten. Temp thirty-nine degrees. No significant medical history but she's had a positive home pregnancy test. Nausea but no vomiting.'

Talia's eyes were open. She was perspiring and looked a little grey.

'Husband is on his way, following behind,' Joe's partner added.

'Doctors?' Joe mouthed the word silently as they wheeled Talia into the hospital.

Kitty shook her head. 'Busy,' she replied, knowing that Joe was thinking they'd need a consult.

Kitty spied Anna coming out of an exam room as they negotiated the corridor. 'Anna! I need a consult if you're free,' Kitty said before Anna could disappear. She let Joe repeat his summary as they transferred Talia to a bed before Kitty and Anna were able to start their assessment.

Kitty started a file and handed it to Anna while she hooked Talia up to the various monitors. Anna recorded Talia's symptoms, the onset and severity, as well as her activities over the previous twenty-four hours and her menstrual history. By Talia's account, she figured she was eight weeks pregnant.

'We'll need a urine sample if that's possible, Talia, just to test and confirm the pregnancy. Kitty, can you organise that? I'll duck out and arrange a pelvic ultrasound.'

Kitty nodded and fetched a bed pan but Anna had gone no further than six steps when Talia cried out in pain. She curled into a ball, clutching her stomach and her heart rate escalated rapidly. She was sweating more profusely and her face was now completely white.

'Anna!' Kitty called out.

Talia wasn't the right demographic for gall stones, which left a burst appendix or a ruptured Fallopian tube as the most likely cause of her pain. That or extremely bad gastro.

Anna came back into the room and took one look at their patient. 'Get me a gynae consult and prep a theatre,' she instructed.

Kitty stripped off her gloves and threw them into the bin as Talia was wheeled off to Theatre. She tidied up the exam room again, and after checking in with Davina and finding that the waiting area was empty she took the opportunity to grab a drink and something to eat. Her shift had been busy and she was finding that if she didn't eat something small on a regular basis the morning sickness would rear its head. It wasn't so much morning sickness as nausea whenever she got hungry and she was quickly learning not to pass up the chance to refuel when she was able to.

Joe was in the kitchen, grabbing a coffee.

'Can I make you one?' he asked.

Kitty shook her head. 'No, thanks, I've gone off coffee.' Her body was already re-

jecting anything that could be considered re-
motely toxic—alcohol, coffee, strong cheeses,
raw fish—and craving healthy options like
fresh fruit and vegetables. She'd always tried
to eat healthily but she was finding it difficult not to now that she was pregnant, as so
many foods made her queasy.

'How did things go with Talia?' Joe asked
as he pulled out a chair for Kitty.

'Not great,' Kitty replied. She pulled the
lid off a tin of tuna and ate a mouthful before continuing. 'She's in Theatre now. Anna
thinks it might have been a ruptured Fallopian tube. I guess she was lucky she was here
and not at home.'

Joe thought Kitty looked worried. A crease
had appeared between her dark brows and
he wondered what was bothering her. She
didn't know Talia, and the woman was far
from the first ED patient who would have
been whisked off to Theatre.

'What's wrong?' he asked.

'I'm just thinking about Talia. There she
was all excited about this pregnancy… It was
her first, did you know that?'

Joe shook his head. There hadn't been the
time or the necessity to go into that detail. It

would have been far different if she'd been in labour, but with an unconfirmed pregnancy it was irrelevant to the ambulance crew.

'One minute she's all excited about the news,' Kitty continued, 'and the next, if Anna's diagnosis is correct, she won't be pregnant any more and the best-case scenario is they are able to save her Fallopian tube. Jess and Cam are so excited about my pregnancy, so excited to meet their child, but I can't stop thinking of all the things that could go wrong.'

So that was the problem. Kitty's imagination was working overtime as usual. She was always of the opinion that if something could go wrong, it would.

'I think I might ask Anna if she can do an ultrasound for me,' she said.

'Why?'

'Just to check things out. It'll make me feel better.'

'You have no reason to think anything is wrong. You've been feeling queasy, you've gone off coffee...' He didn't mention her sore breasts. 'You've got all the right signs.' He knew she had a tendency to worry overly about things and imagine all the things that go awry. 'Have you had another blood test?'

'Yes. My hCG levels are still rising.'

'That's a good sign, right?'

'Yes.'

'When is your scheduled ultrasound?' he asked. He was trying to be the best friend that she expected. He had been consciously trying to stem any negative emotions. Those feelings weren't useful to anyone. But ever since Kitty had confirmed her pregnancy and he'd experienced the unexpected sense of jealousy he had questioned why. And he'd finally figured it out.

Children of his own had never been on his agenda—in his mind if he couldn't commit to a woman he didn't deserve to father children—but with Kitty's announcement he'd had to admit that he actually did want to be a father. He didn't begrudge her the pregnancy, far from it, and it shouldn't matter that she was going to have a baby. That shouldn't impact on his ability to be supportive, and he knew he shouldn't be jealous, but he was finding the reality a little different from the theory. All it did was remind him that someday soon Kitty might be having children of her own, and moving on from their friendship.

But that was *his* issue and he would deal with it, and in the meantime he would make sure he was supportive. Maybe being a surrogate uncle to Kitty's children would suffice.

'Eight days,' she replied.

'I think you should wait until the scan, then. Think of how exciting that is going to be. Don't you want to be able to share that with Jess and Cam? Surely you don't want to take that excitement away from them by having seen it all before?'

She sighed. 'You're right.'

'Good girl. It'll all be fine, you'll see.'

'How come you always know the right thing to say?'

He laughed. 'Maybe to you, because I know you so well.'

'Thanks, Joe.' Kitty stood up and tossed her sandwich wrapper in the bin before hugging him.

He loved the feeling of her arms around him. She was still so tiny and he wondered how long it would be before he'd be able to feel a little baby bump. He didn't imagine it would take long as there was nowhere for the baby to go except out. He wondered too how much the pregnancy would change her. She was worrying now—would she continue to worry progressively more and more throughout the pregnancy, or would she eventually accept that things were going according to plan and relax? Whatever happened, he vowed to be there for her and to help her to cope. He had always been her rock and he didn't want that to change. No matter how he felt.

Kitty was starting to feel more like her normal self. Her morning sickness was abating and, at twenty-two weeks, she was now feeling like she thought she was supposed to—a glowing, pregnant woman. She hadn't gained much weight yet except for in her breasts, but she felt voluptuous for the first time in her life and it was making her feel very feminine. She knew it was hormonal but she was constantly thinking about sex. She hadn't had sex in six months, nearly seven, and she was beginning to think she might go crazy unless she did something about it.

And it seemed she wasn't the only one. As she sat with Lisa and a couple of other nurses at the Manly Pier Hotel the talk turned, inevitably, to men and the lack of good ones.

Kitty was enjoying the evening. It was good to be out and nice to have the focus off the pregnancy for a little while. At home with Jess and Cam it had become the number one topic of conversation, so she was looking forward to talking about the things she used to discuss with her girlfriends. The pub was busy, the line at the bar a couple of people deep. It was her turn to buy the drinks but she didn't feel like fighting her way through the crowd. Like a knight in shining armour Joe appeared and offered to place their order.

'You and Joe aren't an item?' one of the nurses asked, continuing the conversation as she watched Joe walk to the bar.

'No. Just friends,' Kitty replied.

'With benefits?' Victoria asked.

'No.' Kitty shook her head.

'He's hot.'

He did look good tonight, Kitty thought, although she had to pretend she hadn't noticed. He wore his favourite jeans, and they were her favourites on him too. They hugged his backside, highlighting what she considered to be one of his best features. A white

T-shirt hugged his chest. It was a simple out-fit but it showcased his body to perfection. He was fit and muscular with just the right amount of confident swagger, she thought as she watched him leaning on the bar. His hair was casually perfect, he looked like he hadn't made a huge amount of effort, as if he got out of bed looking like this—relaxed and gor-geous with a cheeky grin for whichever fe-male he was talking to.

She had to agree with Victoria. Joe *was* hot, but she'd long ago taught herself to ignore it. They were friends, first and foremost, and she was too afraid of ruining the status quo to ever test the boundaries of that friendship. She needed him as a friend and she wasn't going to risk their relationship by blurring the lines.

'Is he single?' Victoria asked as they watched Joe return to their table.

'He's single,' Kitty admitted.

He delivered their drinks with a smile, making the dimple in his chin flash, and Kitty noticed that Victoria couldn't take her eyes off him. He didn't stay, choosing instead to go out to the deck where some of his mates were drinking, and Victoria's gaze followed his path through the crowd.

All the talk about men and, more specifically Joe, had Kitty flustered. She couldn't think about him and sex in the same conversation. She'd trained herself not to and, besides, he'd never even hinted that he'd be willing to cross that line.

But what if he did? What would she do?

She shook her head.

She'd be crazy to even consider it. She wasn't prepared to risk the friendship of a lifetime for a brief encounter between the sheets. Even if her hormones were going crazy, there were others ways to scratch that itch. Kitty drained her water glass and stood up as the DJ played his first track. The pub was full of good-looking young men. Joe was not the only eligible bachelor here, she thought as she dragged Lisa onto the dance floor.

Joe could see Kitty on the dance floor from his vantage point on the deck. She looked particularly beautiful tonight. He knew she was suffering a little from morning sickness but she had a pregnancy glow and by this evening she was obviously feeling, and looking, better. Her hair was thick and glossy and her skin was luminous. She moved well—she was the epitome of someone who danced as if no one was watching, and he took advantage of that fact to watch her.

She was normally slight, but the pregnancy had added some curves to her bust and her hips, he thought as he watched her hips move to the music. She let herself go to the rhythm of the song and Joe let his eyes follow her movements. There was something hypnotic, almost sensual, about her dancing.

He shook his head and turned away. He felt awkward and exposed now—he wasn't used to thinking about Kitty in that sense. Of course he'd noticed little things about her before—the depth of her brown eyes, the curve of her lips, the twin dimples in her cheeks—but he'd never let himself entertain an image of her as a sexual being before. He'd always kept her firmly in the friend zone.

He turned his gaze to Lisa instead as he tried to get the image of Kitty's hips out of his head and watched as the girls were joined by a couple of guys. Strangers—or at least they were strangers to him. Not that who Kitty danced with was any of his business, but Joe felt his hackles rise anyway as his protective, or should that be territorial, instincts came to the fore.

Kitty danced for a few more minutes but when Lisa's boyfriend arrived she excused herself and headed to the bar, closely followed by one of the guys. Joe's protective instincts kicked up another notch. If this guy wanted a chance with Kitty he'd have to go through him first.

Joe pushed his way through the crowd and arrived at Kitty's side just as the guy asked, 'What can I get you?'

'She'll have a water,' Joe answered.

The guy looked from Kitty to Joe. 'I wasn't asking you.'

'And yet I'm answering.' His protective instincts were on high alert now. Kitty didn't need a stranger buying her drinks, and as the guy half-turned away from Joe to face Kitty, obviously not about to listen to Joe, he couldn't resist adding, 'She's pregnant. She'll have a water.'

He saw the guy glance down at Kitty's stomach. There were no visible signs of her pregnancy yet, not unless you knew her. Joe knew that her breasts were bigger and she was a little softer, a little more rounded, more voluptuous, but she was wearing a loose sleeveless top and jeans. All anyone else would notice was the size of her breasts. And Joe didn't want other guys noticing that.

Her skin glowed. She looked beautiful. And cross.

She was glaring at Joe but he pretended not to notice.

The guy looked back at Joe. He looked irritated too but Joe didn't care. 'Are you the father?' he asked.

'No.'

'Then what business is it of yours?'

'It's her brother-in-law's baby,' Joe stated flatly.

The look on the stranger's face was priceless. If Kitty hadn't still been glaring at him Joe would have laughed. The guy looked completely horrified and he disappeared fast. Just as Joe had hoped.

'What are you doing?' Kitty turned on him.

'What are *you* doing?' he countered.

'I was talking. He was cute.' She was watching him walk away. 'And now he thinks I'm a complete crazy.'

'He wasn't *cute*,' Joe said. 'And he looked

about eighteen. No wonder he ran.' He couldn't help the smile that broke out on his face but Kitty was still cross.

'Joe, I haven't had sex in almost seven months, my hormones are going wild and I'm about to burst with frustration. I wasn't going to marry the guy. It's just sex.'

Just sex.

Joe saw red. He'd never understood that expression until now. Blackness encroached onto the edges of his vision as a red haze washed over the centre. His scientific background told him that it was probably due to a rush of blood through his body, and he would swear he could feel his blood pressure building. He had a burning desire to punch something.

He didn't want to think about Kitty having sex with strangers. The very idea horrified him.

He was aware of other men looking at her with interest and listening to their conversation. He took a deep breath and tried to clear his vision as he gripped her elbow and steered her out to the relative quiet of the deck before any other strangers offered to help her out.

'I was only talking to him,' she argued

again, not prepared to let the discussion drop. 'What's the matter with you?'

'You were talking to him but thinking about sex?' he replied. 'You don't know anything about him.' He knew he sounded like an irrational fool. Kitty was an adult and could make her own decisions, but he really didn't want her thinking about having sex with strangers.

Kitty rolled her eyes. 'If you hadn't scared him off I might have found out more about him. That's how meeting people works, Joe. You meet, you talk, you decide if you like each other.'

'And then you have sex.'

'That was my plan.'

'But you're pregnant.'

'So? You think people don't have sex when they're pregnant?'

He didn't want to think about *her* having sex, pregnant or otherwise. Not with strangers, that was for damn sure.

She was grinning at him now, the little dimples in her cheeks twinkling. He didn't want her to think he was being funny, he was deadly serious. And he wanted her to take him seriously.

He was sorely tempted to offer his services but bit his tongue just in time. There was no way in hell that was a good idea.

She was waiting for his answer. Looking up at him with her big brown eyes, making it difficult to remember just why taking her in his arms and taking her to bed would be so terrible.

'I don't want to talk about you having pregnant sex,' he said as he tried futilely not to imagine what her lips would taste like. Tried not to imagine how her breasts would feel under his fingertips.

'Why not?'

They were standing very close now and the noise from the bar receded into the distance as Kitty continued to look up at him, a challenge in her dark eyes.

Why not what? He couldn't remember what he'd said. He couldn't think straight when she looked at him like that. She was all lips and eyes and breasts and he was a mess.

Their conversation was forgotten as he stared at her lips. He thought about kissing her soundly, showing her what it was like to be kissed by someone who knew her well. Who cared about her. Showing her how much better that was than kissing a complete stranger. Why had he never kissed her before? He couldn't remember.

Everything receded, the noise, the crowd, until there was just the two of them.

He searched for a good reason *not* to kiss her now and couldn't think of one. The urge was overpowering and he didn't know if he could resist.

He bent his head.

She lifted her chin and tilted her head up to him.

CHAPTER FOUR

KITTY'S LIPS WERE PARTED. He could see the tip of her tongue, soft and pink between her teeth. Was she waiting for him to kiss her?

His eyes widened as she licked her lips.

Blood pounded in his veins.

Did she *want* him to kiss her?

How the hell could he know?

Perhaps he was the only one who thought this was a good idea.

No. Scratch that. It was a terrible idea.

He should resist the urge. Although it might be one way to stop her from thinking about sex with strangers... But then where would it leave them?

He was a mess of indecision. He had lost all form of coherent thought and his indecision made him hesitate. In that moment, in that split second when his desire battled with logic, Kitty stepped back.

Her reaction was probably the right one. The best one.

He should also back away before he did something stupid. He'd had several beers and was far from sober. Kissing him was probably the last thing on Kitty's mind. It was highly likely she would have slapped him and he would have deserved it.

He stepped away. That was best. The combination of her hormones and his blood alcohol level may have made them do something they would regret.

He opened his mouth to say something but he was at a loss for words.

Kitty beat him to it. 'I'm tired, I think I might head home,' she said, and she was gone before he could say anything further.

But that was OK. That was good even. That was *definitely* the sensible outcome.

As he watched her go, he tried to gather his thoughts. His brain was fuzzy and it took some time before he could make his legs move.

'Where's Kitty?' Lisa asked as he went back into the pub.

'She's gone home,' he replied. 'She was tired.'

One of the other girls at the table stood up. He recognised her from the hospital, she was one of the nurses. He thought her name was Victoria.

'Would you like to dance?' she asked him. Her voice was quiet and he had to lean in closer to hear her. Had she done that deliberately? She was standing awfully close to him. She was pressed up against his thigh, her hand on his arm, and she was looking at him as if she had no place she needed to be.

Joe didn't dance and he'd had enough to drink. He definitely had somewhere better to be. 'I've got a better idea. Do you want to get out of here?' he said, and was not surprised when she agreed.

Victoria was thin and blonde, the complete opposite of Kitty. She was exactly what he needed to take his mind off what had just happened.

'Kitty and Anna, incoming patient, three minutes,' Davina said. 'I don't have much information. He's a surfer, picked up by the coastguard, suffering from exposure and dehydration. That's all I've got.'

Kitty grabbed a fresh gown and gloves and

made her way to the ambulance bay. Dr Anna
Lewis was already there.

The ambulance pulled in, followed by a
couple of news vans, and Joe jumped out.

Kitty took a deep breath. She hadn't seen
him for several days, not since she'd almost
kissed him, but she'd known their paths
would cross again. She'd also heard that he'd
gone home with Victoria that night. Victoria
had made no secret of that fact the next time
she and Kitty had had a shift together. What
was that all about?

She was still fuming about it. Annoyed
with him and annoyed with herself for car-
ing. She didn't normally have an issue about
Joe's dalliances or relationships, but something about him and Victoria was bugging her
and having to work with Victoria was only
making things worse. She knew it was because she'd stupidly thought he'd been about
to kiss her at the pub. Until he hadn't. Obviously, that had been the last thing on his
mind. He'd probably been about to ask if Victoria was single. Did everyone assume Kitty
would just play matchmaker now that she was
pregnant? Why didn't anyone imagine that

maybe *she* wanted sex? She was pregnant, not dead.

But Kitty had fled the pub after that. She hadn't wanted to give Joe a chance to read what must have been written all over her face. He'd always known what she was thinking and she didn't think she would have managed to hide the fact that she'd thought he'd been about to kiss her—and that she'd desperately wanted him to. What was wrong with her? That would be the surest way to ruin their friendship.

But she still wished he hadn't hooked up with Victoria. That was just rubbing salt into the wound. Victoria was tall and thin and blonde. All the things Kitty wasn't, and Kitty was unusually irritated by the thought of them together.

But there was nothing she could do about it.

Joe pushed the stretcher towards them and Kitty deliberately went to the opposite end, knowing she'd be able to avoid eye contact. She virtually ignored him as he gave them a rundown on the situation while they transferred the patient into an exam room.

Their patient was of Asian appearance,

slim with a badly sunburned nose and shoulders. According to Joe he was Japanese. 'This is Toshi. He got into strife in the surf yesterday and spent the night drifting out to sea on his board.' That caught Kitty's attention but she still avoided looking at Joe and instead looked at Toshi. He'd spent a night in the ocean on a surfboard? 'He is dehydrated, tired and sunburnt but otherwise in reasonable shape considering the circumstances. He's had a litre of saline, this is the second litre running through now. His English is better than my Japanese but I think you should call an interpreter.'

Despite his ordeal, Toshi was able to transfer himself from the stretcher to the examination bed, and Joe smiled at Kitty as he wheeled the stretcher from the room. If he'd noticed her less than friendly attitude towards him it didn't appear to bother him. He wouldn't imagine he'd done anything to upset her and, in reality, she *wouldn't* normally have been upset by his behaviour. He was just being regular Joe. It was hardly his fault she was a hormonal mess.

Kitty hung up the bag of saline and attached leads to Toshi's chest and finger to record his vital statistics. Anna connected him to the oxygen as a precaution but Joe's assessment seemed accurate. Toshi seemed physically in quite a good state, although Kitty wasn't sure what a night spent drifting in the Pacific Ocean would do to a person's mental state. She knew she would have been terrified, imagining sharks circling and all sorts of deadly sea creatures just waiting to pounce. It was just the sort of thing that could lead to PTSD, but there wouldn't be much discussion about Toshi's mental health until the interpreter could be contacted.

'Can you organise some food for him?' Anna asked Kitty when she'd finished her physical examination and declared that he was, indeed, in remarkably good shape. 'Something simple to start with, perhaps soup, a salad and some juice?'

'Sure,' Kitty replied.

'And then we'd better see if we can get an interpreter on the phone if one doesn't turn up shortly. He can have half-hourly obs once he's eaten, providing he keeps something down.'

Kitty organised a tray of food and then took her scheduled break while she waited for it to be delivered. The television in the staff kitchen was on the news channel and Kitty recognised the hospital ED entrance in the background of the shot. A reporter stood in the ambulance bay, speaking to the camera. Kitty wondered if this was the same news crew that had followed the ambulance bringing Toshi. She supposed it was an interesting story.

The emergency doors slid open behind the reporter and Joe stepped outside. Kitty increased the volume when she saw the reporter turn to Joe, thrusting the microphone towards him. Joe stopped, and Kitty wondered if he'd been asked to speak to the media. If so, he was a good choice—after all, he had been one of the paramedics who had transferred Toshi to hospital, and the camera loved him. The angles of his face were thrown into sharp relief by the fluorescent overhead lights of the hospital entrance but his skin still managed to look tanned and healthy and his blue eyes were clear and bright.

'I'm speaking now with one of the paramedics who brought the Japanese surfer here to North Sydney Hospital after his harrowing ordeal lost at sea for sixteen hours,' the young reporter said to the camera, before turning to Joe. 'Mr Harkness, what can you tell us about the man's condition? Is he going to be all right?'

The reporter knew his name, so Joe must have been asked to speak and from past experience Kitty knew it was the only way to get them to move on. You had to give them something otherwise they'd be hovering around all night.

'He was very dehydrated and sunburnt but in remarkably good spirits considering his ordeal. He's understandably relieved to be back on dry land,' Joe replied.

He looked fresh and relaxed. No one would guess he was nearing the end of his twelve-hour shift. The dimple in his chin appeared as he smiled at the young news reporter. Kitty just knew the effect his smile would be having on the young woman. She'd be surprised if she could remember her next question.

'How did he come to be on his surfboard in a shipping lane six kilometres off the east coast of Australia?' the reporter asked, and Kitty was sure she could see a blush colouring her throat as Joe looked directly at her.

'As far as we know, he got dragged out to

sea in a rip and was unable to paddle back in as the waves were too big.'

'And how did he end up in your ambulance?'

'He was spotted by the crew of a container ship and they were able to pick him up. It was fortunate his surfboard was yellow as they may not have seen him otherwise. The coastguard retrieved him and we met them and transferred him here. He's a very lucky man.'

The reporter asked a couple more questions, but Kitty's mind wandered as she watched Joe. She could tell he'd had enough of being interviewed. He was still being pleasant but the set of his shoulders had changed. He was angled away from the reporter now and although Kitty couldn't see his feet she suspected he had shifted his weight. He'd be getting ready to move. She could read his body language, knew his movements. She had spent so much time with him, watching him, she knew the set of his head, the curve of his cheek, the exact position of the dimple in his chin. She didn't want to be cross with him. She acknowledged that it stemmed from being irritated with herself. It wasn't his fault she was hormonal.

She felt a flutter in her belly as the baby stretched and moved and reminded her of what was important. Family. Friends. Joe was as important to her as anyone. She'd mend the bridges.

She didn't get to choose who Joe spent his time with. That was all up to him and he'd obviously not wanted to kiss her. Thank God when he'd bent his head towards her that night at the pub she hadn't met him halfway—she would have died of embarrassment. As it was, it was bad enough that he'd hooked up with Victoria. Had that been his plan all along for that night?

She remembered he'd asked her not to talk about pregnant sex. Did he think her pregnancy made her unattractive? Undesirable?

Had she just *imagined* that he was going to kiss her? Had she wanted him to?

She knew she had. Did.

But perhaps it was best that she hadn't. She needed him in her life and she couldn't afford to jeopardise their relationship. He was one of the few people she could rely on to have her back. She couldn't risk altering the status quo.

So she'd better stop being in a huff about Victoria. She didn't need to socialise with them as a couple but she should stop ignoring Joe.

Even Jess had noticed that Joe hadn't been around for the past few days. Kitty's birthday was next week and she had always celebrated it with Joe. Jess and Cam had been pressuring her to invite him for dinner. She checked the roster. She wanted to know which nights Victoria was working. She could invite Joe and feign ignorance that Victoria had a shift.

She went out to the ambulance bay, anxious to catch Joe before he left. Suddenly she felt it was important to fix things. To act like an adult.

She waited until the reporter signed off on her segment and the news crew had started packing up their gear before she hurried after him.

'Joe? Can I talk to you?'

'Hey.' He turned around with a smile. He looked pleased to see her. Maybe he hadn't even noticed she'd been avoiding him. He was probably too caught up in Victoria to have time to think about her. She pushed those thoughts aside. She didn't want to think about Victoria any more than she had to, and basked in the warmth of Joe's smile instead. 'How are you?' he asked. 'How's our patient?'

'Hungry.' She smiled back. 'Toshi, I mean,' she clarified.

'That's a good sign.'

'It is,' she agreed. 'I saw your interview.'

'Is that what you came to tell me? Was it terrible?'

She shook her head. 'You know it wasn't. I wanted to ask if you are free for dinner tomorrow night? Cam is going to make a barbecue,' she said, reminding herself she'd have to remember to tell Cam. 'It's an early birthday celebration for me. Would you like to come over?'

'Sounds great.'

'You're welcome to bring Victoria,' she offered, hoping that Joe would already know she had a shift and wouldn't ask her to swap it.

'Thanks, but I don't think we're at that point in our relationship yet.'

'OK.' Kitty did a mental fist pump. That had worked out well—she'd looked gracious while still getting what she wanted. Joe hadn't even thought about checking Victoria's roster. 'See you at seven.'

That was good. He didn't seem out of sorts with her. She didn't want to push him away, to give him a reason to abandon their friendship, abandon her. Everyone left her eventually but she really wanted to keep Joe in her life for as long as possible. She needed him.

Kitty answered Joe's knock on the door. She was wearing a dress he hadn't seen before. She looked good. Pink suited her. She was glowing, making him wonder suddenly if she'd had the sex she'd been seeking out the other night. Had sex put the sparkle in her eyes and the glow on her cheeks?

He didn't want to think about Kitty having sex. Not if it wasn't with him. But that wasn't going to happen, and thinking about it wasn't going to do anyone any good.

'New dress?' he asked as he kissed her cheek and handed her the gifts he'd brought.

'I had to go shopping. I don't fit into my clothes any more,' she said as she led him into the house. His gaze dropped to her hips, which were swaying tantalisingly in front of him. This pregnancy had filled her out, rounding her bottom, in a good way, and Joe felt a corresponding tightness in his groin.

He greeted Jess and Cam and handed Cam a six-pack of beer as he tried to ignore the stirring of lust that threatened to destroy his concentration.

'Good man. I'm living in a teetotaller house these days. I'm trying to be supportive and it's no fun drinking without company,' Cam said as he cracked the tops of a couple of the small bottles and handed one back to Joe. 'Jess isn't drinking either.'

'I'm keeping Kitty company,' she said.

'How many weeks are you now?' Joe asked Kitty. 'Twenty-two?'

'Twenty-four.'

His question had purely been conversational. He knew exactly how many weeks she was.

'We had a scan today,' Jess told him. He thought it was strange that she said 'we'. He knew that genetically the baby was hers and she obviously felt a connection but Kitty was the one who was pregnant. 'Would you like to see the picture?' Jess asked.

'Sure.'

'I'm not sure that Joe is as interested in our baby as we are,' Cam told his wife.

'It's fine,' Joe said, trying to sound enthusiastic.

Jess went to the fridge and removed a small square black and white picture from where it had been held in place by a magnet. She held it out to Joe.

This was OK. He'd seen plenty of ultrasound scans before. It was just a baby. As long as he didn't think that this baby was responsible for the change in Kitty's shape and the subsequent change in his perception of her it was all good. At this stage, it just looked like any baby. With a perfect profile, sucking its thumb.

'Do you know if it's a boy or a girl?' he asked.

Jess shook her head. 'We can't agree. I want to know, but Cam—'

'I want a surprise,' Cam said, finishing Jess's sentence for her as she started coughing. Cam fetched her a glass of water and Jess drank it in fits and starts, between coughs, until she could speak again.

'I want to know because I want to decorate the nursery. If we're only going to do this once I'd like time to be prepared.'

Joe suspected that meant that they *would*

find out the sex. In his experience the woman got her way in these things. But who would have the final say? Who would the doctor listen to? Technically, Kitty was the mother. What would she say? He didn't want to ask that question. He decided to stick to a safer topic. 'Only once, you say?'

'I'd be happy with one,' Cam said. 'It's one more than we thought we'd have.'

'I'd like more, but I'm not going to be greedy,' Jess admitted.

'Let's just get this one here safely,' Cam said.

'I know, I'm not going to get ahead of myself but I loved growing up with a sister. I couldn't do this without her,' Jess said as she took the ultrasound picture back from Joe and hugged Kitty, 'and I'd like to think of my own children having the same relationship with a sibling.'

Joe had brothers and sisters, but none of them were full siblings, and he certainly didn't share the bond with any of them like Kitty and Jess had. 'There's no guarantee that they'd get along, you know. I've got five siblings and I don't really get along with any of them.' In fact, he had always thought Kitty was more like a sister than his real ones. Until the past week at least, when he'd started having very unfamilial thoughts about her.

'I find that hard to believe,' Cam said. 'I picked you as one of those blokes that gets on with everyone.'

Joe laughed. 'Maybe that says more about me than them.'

Kitty came to his defence. 'You're not really close in age to any of them and you didn't really grow up together. That makes a difference.'

'I guess what I'm saying is that I grew up virtually as an only child, and in a lot of ways I think I had a happier childhood for it.' His teenage years maybe hadn't been quite so happy, but that was because he'd been old enough to realise that he didn't really fit in with any of his families. But that wasn't because he didn't have siblings—that was because his mum and dad hadn't been able to stay married. To anyone. And that had meant he'd constantly had his boundaries and his living arrangements changed around him, completely out of his control. He hadn't like that and had become rebellious, which had made him difficult to live with. Not just for his parents but probably for some of his brothers and sisters, too. It was circumstances that had made him.

'I didn't know you were one of six,' Jess said.

'Two half-siblings and three step-siblings. In some ways I'm surprised it's not more. My parents divorced when I was four. Mum was Dad's second wife, but they've both been married three times now. That's a lot of families to juggle and a lot of different dynamics. I think I preferred it when I was on my own. In a lot of ways it made life easier.'

Joe didn't think much of a typical family unit but he knew his reservations were due to watching his parents struggle to keep marriages together. Although struggle wasn't the right word—neither of them really seemed to put much effort into making their marriages last. They both seemed to prefer just to give up and move on to the next one. Joe knew that Kitty and Jess had grown up in a stable family unit, at least until tragedy had taken both their parents when Kitty had been nineteen, and he could understand why they expected to have the same stable environment. But in his experience that was virtually impossible. The impossible dream.

'I think we'll just take this one step at a time. One baby at a time,' Cam said as he kissed his wife. 'And see how we manage.'

Joe thought Cam's logic was practical and sensible. There were a lot of unknowns in Cam and Jess's future. The new baby was only one of them.

Dinner was finished—steak and a glass of red wine for Cam and Joe, fish and lime-flavoured sparkling mineral water for Jess and Kitty. Cam cleared the plates and said to Joe, 'Come and join me for a beer while I clean the barbecue.'

Joe followed him over to the grill and took a swig of his beer. 'Do you think this surrogacy thing is a good idea?' he asked as he stood watching Cam work. 'Actually, scratch that. You must.'

Cam didn't answer immediately. 'It's what Jess wanted. I love my wife. I want her to be happy and this is what she wanted. I didn't have the same burning desire to have children. Don't get me wrong, I'm not against the idea, but if it didn't happen for us I was OK with that. But Jess wants kids. I'm doing this for her. That's what love is all about.'

Joe figured he wouldn't know anything about all that but all the same his gaze was drawn to Kitty. He could see her through the window. She was standing by the kettle, pulling mugs off the shelf.

'Speaking of love…' Cam's voice made Joe jump. He dragged his eyes off Kitty and back to Cam, wondering where he was going with this topic, but Cam was scraping the barbecue, seemingly disinterested in who or what Joe was watching. 'Kitty tells me you're seeing someone. Is it serious?'

Joe almost choked. 'God, no. I try to avoid serious relationships.'

'Maybe you just haven't met the perfect girl yet,' Cam said, echoing the words of so many of Joe's friends, but Joe thought differently.

'No one's perfect,' he said, 'and nothing lasts for ever. I don't see the point in starting something that won't last.'

Even Cam and Jess's relationship, as perfect as it might look from the outside, had its downsides in Joe's opinion. Jess's cancer and inability to get pregnant was far from their idea of perfect. But Joe wasn't about to make an example of Cam's own marriage as his argument.

'What about Kitty?'

'Kitty?'

'Is that so hard to imagine? You and Kitty? You must like her.'

'Of course I like her, she's my best friend.'

He'd been trying to remind himself of that every day since he'd nearly succumbed to temptation and almost kissed her. He continued to tell himself he was glad he'd resisted. That would have been disastrous.

'C'mon, Joe. You don't think Jess and I haven't talked about this? We think you guys would be good together.'

Joe wasn't so sure. As tempted as he had been the other night, he was still convinced that a quick tumble between the sheets would have been a sure way to ruin their friendship. But that hadn't stopped him thinking about it. And opting to take Victoria home that night instead hadn't stopped him thinking about it either. But thinking about it was one thing, acting on it was another thing altogether, and there were dozens of reasons why he would steer clear. Starting with the biggest one—

he and Kitty wanted different things out of relationships.

'I'm not the right man for her,' he said. 'Kitty is looking for someone who can commit to her, someone who will promise to never leave her. I don't believe in happily ever after. We'd be a terrible combination.'

'You think?'

Joe nodded. He'd given this a lot of thought over the past couple of weeks, and no matter how much he might wish things had turned out differently he knew he wasn't the right man for Kitty. He was not what Kitty needed. 'Trust me, I'm not the man she needs and I really don't want to ruin a perfectly good friendship.'

Cam laughed. 'There's no such thing as a friendship between a man and a woman. You've heard that saying. Men will always muck it up by wanting sex.'

Cam definitely had a point, but Joe couldn't agree with him. He was desperate to bring this conversation to an end before he admitted to something that had disaster written all over it. 'Wanting and having are two different things, my friend,' he said, 'and it's the having that mucks things up. Better Kitty and I stick to what we do best. It's worked for us so far.'

'OK, mate, whatever you say.' Cam's expression was sceptical as he covered the barbecue and knocked the lids off a couple more beers.

Joe knew he didn't believe him, and he couldn't blame Cam. Even Joe was not convinced, but he knew he couldn't give in to his desires no matter how much he wanted to. He really couldn't risk ruining his relationship with Kitty over his crazy ideas. Surely, given time, he'd get this ridiculous feeling out of his system and life would go on with Kitty being none the wiser.

Twenty-eight weeks. Only twelve to go.

Kitty was no longer thinking of her life in terms of days of the week or even months of the year—everything had been reduced to weeks of her pregnancy and the associated milestones. At twenty-eight weeks she was two-thirds of the way there. The baby was putting on weight, her skin was filling out and she was constantly on the move.

Last week she had volunteered to be a patient at one of the student sonography clinics held at the hospital and she had asked to find out the baby's sex. She was having a girl.

But she had hugged that knowledge to herself. She'd had to share every little piece of this pregnancy with Jess and Cam, and for the most part she'd been happy to do that, but it was nice to have something that was hers alone. She felt a little guilty about keeping the secret, and on occasion she'd had to be careful with her language to ensure she didn't use 'she' in reference to the baby too often. An occasional mention could be passed off as a figure of speech but she had to remember to use 'he' at times too. But in her opinion there was no harm in having this one secret. It wasn't going to hurt anyone.

Cam didn't want to know the baby's sex and Kitty knew it was better to keep her secret than to risk spoiling the surprise for Cam. And not knowing hadn't stopped Jess from starting to decorate the nursery. She had gone for a white palette with pretty pale apple green accents, which she said she could team with pink or navy depending on whether the baby was a boy or a girl.

The baby kicked as if knowing Kitty was thinking about her. She put a hand on her belly and smiled. She was happy. She was doing a good thing for her sister, growing a beautiful baby—and she'd even patched things up with Joe. Things were back on an even keel with him since her birthday dinner. As far as she knew, he was still seeing Victoria but she was trying not to let that bother her. She'd avoided going out with the hospital staff since that night. She used fatigue and the fact that she wasn't drinking as her excuse, but she really didn't want to put herself in a situation where she would have to see Joe and Victoria together. As long as she didn't have to see them together she could pretend it wasn't happening. Ignorance might not be bliss but it was better than the alternative.

And she *was* finding work tiring. Being on her feet for hours on end while carrying around an extra six kilograms was exhausting. She hadn't put on a lot of weight but six kilograms was just the beginning and it felt like a lot on her small frame, meaning she was happy to spend most nights on the couch.

She was due for a break and, unlike her pre-pregnancy days when she'd often skipped or shortened her breaks, now she looked forward to them and made sure she sat down for a few minutes to give her feet and ankles a rest. Her Saturday night shift had been busy and she didn't expect it to get any quieter. She grabbed a sandwich and a piece of fruit from her locker and took it outside.

To her left she spotted Joe, sitting on the retaining wall that separated the garden bed from the ambulance bay. Victoria was standing in front of him, partially obscuring Kitty's view, but she only needed a glimpse to know it was him. Kitty tried to ignore the feelings of jealousy that swamped her. She hated feeling jealous, but she hated seeing Joe with Victoria even more. She was still blaming her hormones even though she knew it was really about the almost-kiss. She was having trouble forgetting that.

She'd been an idiot. She'd nearly ruined their friendship. Of course he'd hesitated. She'd crossed their boundaries. She was relieved that he didn't seem to be holding her faux pas against her, but she couldn't forget it and she couldn't deny that she wanted to know what it would be like to kiss him properly. She'd been dreaming about it. All her searching on the internet had reinforced the idea that her hormones were running wild in this trimester but she couldn't help but think it was more than that. She couldn't get the idea out of her head. She wasn't having fantasies about any other men. Just Joe.

She contemplated going back into the hospital but she really wanted some fresh air. She bit into her apple as she turned right, away from Joe. She didn't think he'd seen her and she certainly didn't want to see the two of them together. It made her feel lonely and diminished her happiness. Jess had Cam and Joe had Victoria, but she had no one.

As if to cheer her up, the baby somersaulted in her womb. She was active tonight, Kitty thought as she put her hand on her stomach. She wasn't alone, not right now, but even the baby was only hers temporarily. This pregnancy was of her choosing, it was what she wanted, but she knew that, ultimately, she wanted to be part of a couple. She wanted to be loved. She wanted a family of her own one day. But for now she needed to focus on the pregnancy and hope that her time would come.

She finished her sandwich and wrapped the apple core in the left-over packaging, then with one final glance in Joe's direction she went back into the hospital. She threw her rubbish in a bin at the triage desk and went to wash her hands, glancing around the waiting area as she dried them. The ED waiting area was empty, the ED quiet; Lisa was the only staff member Kitty could see, which meant that all the other staff were busy in treatment rooms or were taking their breaks. Kitty was walking towards the desk when the entrance doors slid open, admitting a very thin, dishevelled man in a pair of dirty jeans and a grubby T-shirt. Scabs covered his forearms and he was scratching at them agitatedly. He scanned the department as he entered. His eyes were wide, his pupils dilated, and his movements were jerky and frantic. Kitty recognised that look. The familiar look of a methamphetamine user.

His gaze landed on Kitty and he started yelling as he advanced towards her in an unnatural, nervous gait.

'Help me! They're tracking me, they're going to kill me!' His scratching gathered intensity and he had picked off several scabs. His arms were now bleeding.

Kitty was stranded on the wrong side of the desk. The desk was separated from the waiting area by a glass window and access to it was via a pair of doors that needed a security code to open. The desk resembled a bank counter. Lisa was the teller, safely barricaded behind the glass, but Kitty was exposed and vulnerable. She wanted to seek refuge but she was afraid to move, worried that any movement might trigger a reaction in this man. A reaction she wasn't at all keen to witness.

She reached slowly into the pocket of her scrubs and retrieved a pair of surgical gloves, pulling them on carefully as she glanced at Lisa, knowing they needed back-up and knowing Lisa would push the button to call for help.

She reached out a hand, silently begging him to stop, praying that back-up would arrive before he got to her. 'It's all right, no one is going to hurt you here. You're safe.'

He continued to look around but he stopped walking. He'd stopped almost level with the door that Kitty could have escaped through. If he took one more step in her direction he would effectively block her access to safety.

Kitty had to risk it. She knew Lisa could push another button that would open the door and let her in, once Kitty got close enough. She looked at her. Lisa nodded and moved towards the button as Kitty moved towards the door. Towards the man.

'Stay away from me!'

Kitty froze. He'd taken her movement as a threat.

She raised her hands, intending to convey she meant him no harm. Her heart was in her mouth and she could feel every beat echoing through her body. Adrenalin coursed through her, triggering her fight or flight response. She wanted to flee but there was nowhere to go. This man was blocking her escape route, and the only thing between him and her was her pregnant belly.

She couldn't risk it. She had to get out of there. She was terrified, afraid to turn her back, but she had no other option. She was trapped. She couldn't go forward. She could only go back.

Kitty slid back a step, but he took another lurch forward.

'What are you doing?' he yelled at her.

She hesitated. She didn't want to upset him. He was drug fuelled, erratic and unpredictable. Who knew what he was capable of?

Kitty took her eyes off him momentarily, searching to see if help was coming in any form. Surely minutes must have passed since Lisa had pressed the alarm? Where was everyone?

He was watching her. 'Who's there? Is it them?' He turned his head to look over his shoulder and Kitty took another step backwards but she wasn't fast enough. He had turned back to face her, catching her movement.

He advanced towards her, reaching behind his back as he walked. Kitty froze. She was terrified.

He brought his hand forward and Kitty's eyes went wide. He was holding a large knife. Light reflected off the blade, glinting ominously.

Kitty couldn't move. She was so frightened she'd lost voluntary control of her limbs, her muscles stiff and unresponsive.

He lunged at her, and Kitty was surprised by the speed of his movement and the power of his skinny body. She felt a blow to her chest that was hard enough to knock the wind from her lungs. She felt herself falling, and the last thing she remembered was the shine of the overhead fluorescent lights reflecting off the blade of his knife.

CHAPTER FIVE

JOE HAD SEEN Kitty come out of the hospital. Out of the corner of his eye he'd seen her glance his way as he sat with Victoria, and seen her choose not to come and say hello. Things between them had been a little strained for the past few weeks. If he'd had to put a time frame to when it had started he would pick the night at the pub. The night he'd almost kissed her.

Not that she'd said anything. Nothing had been said about it by either of them, and he had to assume he was the only one dwelling on it. That he was the only one who considered it a missed opportunity. He wasn't sure that Kitty had even realised what he'd been so tempted to do. For all he knew, she had been, and still was, oblivious to the whole episode—but it didn't explain how she was behaving.

He'd thought that things might be back to normal when she'd invited him to her birthday dinner but there was still tension between them. He could feel it. And she was definitely avoiding him. She'd made excuses about why she couldn't catch up with him. She'd blamed the pregnancy—she was tired or had appointments—but he wasn't convinced that was the sole reason. He wasn't certain it was to do with the almost-kiss but *something* wasn't right.

Maybe he *should* have kissed her. Maybe that would have brought things to a head and sorted it out once and for all. God knew, he'd spent far too long thinking about the missed opportunity, and he'd thought the best way to get her out of his head was to date someone else but even that wasn't working.

He wished she'd never mentioned wanting sex. He wished she wasn't pregnant and full of raging hormones. Hormones that made her think of random sex with strangers and, in turn, made him think of sex with her. He wished things had stayed the same. But he was having a hard time thinking of her in a platonic sense now. Since she'd talked about wanting sex and his conversation with

Cam, all he could think about was 'could it work?' But he knew, realistically, it couldn't. It wouldn't. It would be an unmitigated disaster. He'd mess it up for sure.

But that didn't stop him from dreaming and wishing and imagining. It hadn't stopped him from watching her out of the corner of his eye as she'd sat and eaten and very carefully avoided looking at him.

He knew she'd seen him, and he'd kept an eye on her even as he'd tried to continue his discussion with Victoria. He'd been busy trying to tell her that their relationship wasn't going to work without really explaining why. He couldn't, in good conscience, continue to sleep with her when his head was full of thoughts about making love to someone else. Not even if he knew that was never going to happen. Because the short answer was he couldn't be with Kitty. He'd meant it when he'd told Cam he wasn't the man Kitty needed.

But he'd still kept one eye on her as Victoria had railed at him and called him heartless, and even while she'd accused him of not listening to her or paying attention. He hadn't admitted she was right.

He'd seen Kitty glance their way and choose to head in the opposite direction, and he'd seen her finish eating and disappear back inside the hospital. And, because he'd still been watching the entrance to the ED, he'd noticed a tall, thin man approaching the entrance, too. The man had been dishevelled and talking to himself, and Joe's antennae had pricked.

He'd looked distressed and when Joe saw the guy go into the ED he followed, his suspicions alerted.

The ED doors slid open as they sensed him and Joe stepped inside and found himself in the midst of his worst nightmare.

The ED was virtually empty but despite the lack of people there was noise, chaos and confusion. It was out of proportion considering the emptiness of the space.

Movement to his right caught his eye.

Someone was falling. Fast. He saw their head hit the wall and saw them land in a crumpled heap.

And then he saw that the someone was Kitty.

The guy Joe had followed into the ED was moving towards her and Joe started running before he'd fully taken stock of the situation. All he knew was that he had to get to Kitty.

He sprinted towards her.

Subconsciously he registered that the guy wasn't distressed. He was high.

Joe had seen what methamphetamines could do to people. He'd witnessed the rage it could induce, the psychotic episodes and the physical violence that ensued, and all he could think about was getting to Kitty before this guy did. He didn't stop to think about what he was going to do. He'd seen it take four big men to subdue meth addicts before. He'd been one of those guys holding them down plenty of times so he knew the super-human strength the drug imparted and there was no way he was going to let this guy harm Kitty. Not more than he already had.

'Hey!' he yelled. He had to distract him. The man turned and Joe reached out, instinctively trying to placate him. It was a ridiculous idea as he was obviously high, but Joe's only thought was to get him away from Kitty. 'What are you doing?'

The guy was still spinning, turning at the sound of Joe's voice. 'Stay away from me.' His rancid breath assailed Joe's senses and his pupils were so dilated that his eyes looked like two dark holes in his face. He lashed out at Joe as he turned. Joe felt a searing pain in his hand and saw the light bouncing off a steel blade.

A knife.

He hadn't anticipated that.

He tried to skid to a stop but his momentum carried him forward, straight into the path of the blade.

Pain burst through his abdomen.

The pain was similar to getting punched in the stomach and Joe had time to think it was strange—he'd always expected knifing pain to be sharp. He pushed the man away from him with a force he hadn't known he had, and as the man stumbled backwards Joe looked down. The pain wasn't excruciating. Maybe he hadn't just been stabbed?

He put his hand over his stomach and it came away covered in blood. He could feel it now, warm and wet and sticky, soaking into his dark blue uniform.

Ahead of him, over the man's right shoulder, Joe saw four of the hospital security staff arrive, followed by one of the ED doctors. The security guards threw a net over the man, who bucked and thrashed like a wild animal. It took all four guards to hold him down.

As Joe watched the man kicking and screaming under the net, red and blue light bathed the walls of the ED, flashing on and off and making the experience a little surreal as police cars pulled up to the department doors. The police rushed in, tasers in hand and guns holstered, but Joe could see that their holsters were unclipped and ready for whatever happened next. Joe knew they would have been through this process before. They all had. This was nothing new in hospital emergency departments country-wide.

But the police were not the front line this time. The security guards had managed to contain the man. They had his hands pinned behind his back but he continued to resist. Two policeman joined in as they attempted to subdue him, attempted to get him into a position where the doctor could administer a sedative. Six big men and one doctor. All to contain one drug user. And meanwhile Kitty was still lying sprawled against the wall. She hadn't moved and no one had been near her. No one had so much as glanced her way. There was no one spare.

There was only him.

He had to help her.

He took a step towards her but his knees buckled under him, surprising him, and he found himself kneeling on the floor in a pool of his own blood.

He was bent double and it hurt to breathe, but at least he *was* still breathing. His left hand was pressed against his stomach, just below his ribs, and he could feel his lungs inflate and deflate. His stomach muscles screamed and his right hand throbbed, but he was alive and breathing. Kitty still hadn't moved.

He moved his left hand, placing it on the floor to stabilise himself. He pressed his right elbow into his side and applied pressure to his abdominal wound as he crawled across the floor to Kitty, leaving a trail of blood in his wake.

She was still slumped against the wall. She was pale and her eyes were closed. He could see the small bump of her pregnancy under the blue fabric of her scrubs and he could see the rise and fall of her chest just above the bump. He let out a sigh of relief and some of the tension he'd been holding dissolved with the sigh. She was breathing.

He knelt beside her and reached out, putting his left hand on her shoulder. He winced in pain as the movement stretched his stomach.

'Kitty, can you hear me? Open your eyes.' He shook her shoulder, very gently, and his hand left a bloody print on her top. 'Kitty?' he repeated, and he could hear the desperation in his voice.

There was no response.

'I need some help here,' he called over his shoulder. The sound was loud in his ears, echoing off the walls that were still bathed in blue and red lights from the police cruisers, but there was no reaction. Everyone was busy.

He knew only seconds had passed since he'd stepped inside the ED, even though it felt like an eternity, but Kitty needed help. She needed a doctor.

Joe looked up and saw Anna on the far side of the department and called her by name. He saw her turn in his direction. He could see as she registered all the blood and hurried over to him.

'Not me,' he said as Anna knelt beside him,

assuming he was the one who needed help. 'Check Kitty. She's non-responsive.' He knew he needed medical attention, but in his mind Kitty's need was greater. She was living for two.

'Kitty, can you hear me?'
    Joe?
A bright flash of light startled her but as she lifted one hand to block it out it disappeared, only to reappear again a moment later. She felt her eyelids drop and the light went out again.

'Left pupil sluggish.'

'Kitty? Can you hear me? It's Anna Lewis.'
    Anna? She was sure she'd heard Joe's voice. What was going on?

'Kitty, open your eyes.'

She opened her eyes and saw the ED doctor squatting in front of her. Why were they both on the floor?

Kitty could hear Anna talking to her and she tried to focus, tried to concentrate on Anna's words. 'You fell and hit your head. We're going to put you on a stretcher and take you to be examined.'

Kitty frowned as she tried to work out what

was going on. She felt pressure on her arm, someone was wrapping a blood-pressure cuff around it. She turned her head but the movement made her wince as pain stabbed behind her eyes. She lifted her hand to her head. There was a massive lump at the back of her skull and she had a killer headache.

She closed her eyes as bile rose in her throat. 'I think I'm going to be sick.'

Someone thrust a green bowl towards her, just in time, and Kitty retched into the plastic container.

She lifted her head as she finished vomiting but the pain hadn't eased. If anything, vomiting had made her head throb even more. Out of the corner of one eye she could see someone being restrained by half a dozen men—cops and security guards crowded the ED but she resisted the temptation to turn her head to get a better look, not game to risk more pain. She closed her eyes as the pressure inside her head increased. It felt like her head was on the verge of exploding. The ED was chaotic. Noisy and crowded. People were yelling and moving past quickly. She just wanted some peace and quiet. She just wanted to sleep.

She felt the blood-pressure cuff being loosened around her arm. Heard someone say, 'BP one-sixty over one hundred.'

'Kitty? I need you to open your eyes. I need you to stay awake.' She heard Anna speaking to her. She didn't want to open her eyes. She didn't want to do anything. But she forced one eye open, and then the other. She sensed it was important to do as Anna asked.

Her eyes focussed on a pool of blood on the floor next to her. Where had that come from? Was it hers?

And then she remembered.

The baby!

'Anna?' She pointed to the blood as she struggled to speak. Her tongue felt swollen and her mouth was dry. She struggled to form even a simple word. Her heart pounded in her chest and she could feel the accompanying thump in her brain. 'The baby?'

'Don't worry, it's not your blood,' Anna said.

'Whose…?'

'It's Joe's.'

Another wave of nausea engulfed her and black spots swarmed in front of her eyes as her vision blurred. She resisted the urge to close her eyes and give in. *Joe's?* What had happened? What had happened to Joe? She needed to know how he was. *Where* he was. She looked around the ED but moving her head hurt, and moving her eyes wasn't any better. The nausea intensified and the black spots multiplied and were accompanied now by a ringing in her ears, and as the chaos and noise continued around her she succumbed to the fatigue.

Images flashed through Kitty's brain like drawings in a flip book, but instead of evolving into something recognisable the pictures were jumbled, nonsensical and fleeting. Too fleeting to grab hold of and decipher. There were snippets of conversation, flashes of light and a sensation of falling but nothing that made sense. Her head throbbed and her body ached. She felt battered and bruised but couldn't figure out why.

Her left elbow was sore and when she opened her eyes she could see an IV line snaking its way into her vein.

'Hi. I was wondering when you'd wake up.' Lisa stood at the end of the bed, having moved into the line of Kitty's vision. 'You caused quite a commotion.'

'I did?' Kitty frowned. 'What happened? What am I doing here?'

'You don't remember?'

Kitty shook her head before realising that was a bad idea. 'No,' she said.

'This guy came into the ED, high on methamphetamines, yelling about how "they" were after him. He shoved you. You fell and hit your head and then Joe came in like an avenging angel and—'

'Joe?' Kitty remembered someone saying something about him.

'Yes. He managed to distract the guy, to stop him from assaulting you further, but he was attacked. The guy had a knife.'

A knife! Kitty's heart rate escalated as she remembered the blood. All that blood. It was Joe's. 'Is he all right? Joe? Is he all right?'

'You should have seen him, Kitty. He was amazing. He saved your life.'

Her headache was getting worse. She needed Lisa to stop talking but first she needed an answer. 'Lisa, is Joe OK?'

'He was stabbed,' Lisa said, but she was nodding. 'In the stomach. He had to go into Theatre, but he's out now.'

Kitty breathed out.

'Can you take me to him?' She was exhausted and sore but she had an overwhelming desire to see him.

'I don't think you're allowed to be moved,' Lisa said, just as Anna came into the room.

'You need to rest, Kitty,' she told her, making it clear she'd heard the last part of the conversation.

'I want to see Joe.'

'Joe is going to be fine. You need to rest.'

She didn't think she'd be able to rest, not until she'd seen Joe.

'Jess and Cam are on their way,' Anna continued, 'and the baby needs you to rest. I'm not arguing about this.'

'The baby—'

'Is fine.'

Kitty realised she had instinctively put one hand on her belly. It had become a habit. She held it there, waiting, hoping, needing to feel some movement. 'Are you sure?'

'We did an ultrasound. The baby is fine,' Anna repeated, just as Kitty felt the baby kick. She had a vague recollection of being moved and lifted. Had that been for the scans?

'You need monitoring,' Anna said. 'Your blood pressure is still high and if it doesn't come down I'll need to administer hydralazine, and I am going to arrange a CT scan of your head too. Your baby is fine but I'm sure you want to keep it that way?'

Kitty nodded carefully, agreeing with Anna. But only for her baby's sake.

Joe opened his eyes. The room was dark and it wasn't his room.

Was it morning or night?

He could remember being woken but couldn't remember where he was.

He could hear electronic beeping. Turning his head, he could see monitors beside the bed.

A hospital bed.

He tried to sit up but pain knifed through his abdominals, making him gasp. He clutched his stomach with his right hand and gasped again as pain sliced through his hand as well.

He looked down and saw that his right hand was bandaged, and the memories flooded back. The man. A knife. Kitty!

He tried again to sit up. He needed to find out if Kitty was OK, but the pain in his stomach screamed at him not to move. He lifted the bed sheet with his left hand and saw the dressing on his stomach. He let the sheet fall and rested his head on the pillow.

He should have known better. He'd seen plenty of patients high on drugs and he'd seen first-hand the inhuman strength the drug gave them. He should have known better, but he hadn't stopped to think about that this time. All he'd been able to think about was Kitty. All he'd *seen* was Kitty, lying motionless on the floor, with a manic fool headed straight for her.

The clock on the monitor beside his bed said six-thirty and the light around the edge of the window blinds in the room looked like morning, but he had no clue as to what day it was or how long he'd been there.

The call bell was pinned to the left side of his bed. He pressed the button for the nurse.

'Good morning. Back in the land of the living, I see,' the nurse said as she came into the room.

Morning.

That was one question answered.

Joe scanned the nurse's ID badge. *North Sydney Hospital*. The name 'Paula' was typed under her photo. He hadn't moved far. Just upstairs onto a ward.

He frowned. 'How long have I been here?' He held up his bandaged hand. 'And what have they done to me?'

'You were brought to the ward from Recovery last night. You had a deep stab wound to your right abdomen. You had emergency surgery to clean it out and close it up.'

'What about my hand?'

'You've been referred to Dr Clark, she's a hand surgeon, she'll discuss that with you. Now, what can I help you with? Do you need something? More pain relief?' The nurse picked up the tubing that was feeding pain relief through Joe's arm into his body. He'd seen the monitors but hadn't noticed the IV pump.

'I don't need pain relief but can you find out about a nurse who works here. Kitty Nelson? She was injured in the ED in the same incident as me. Do you know if she's OK?'

'Are you her next of kin?'

'No.' His heart leapt and lodged in his throat. Why was she asking about Kitty's next of kin? 'What happened to her?'

'You know I can't tell you about other patients.'

'Please,' he begged. He had to know if she was all right. He had to know she'd made it.

Paula was older than Joe, closer to forty than thirty, and he doubted his charms would work on her. She'd probably seen and heard it all before. A young nurse would no doubt be more accommodating but he had to try. 'I got into this mess by trying to protect her. I need to know if she's all right.' Paula wore a wedding ring so he tried appealing to her sense of romance, hoping she was happily married to someone who would protect her if necessary.

She looked at him and he smiled. There was no point in pretending he wasn't trying to get her on side.

'OK, I'll see what I can find out.'

It was only when Paula left that he realised he should have asked about the baby too. But, if he was honest, the baby wasn't his concern. Kitty was.

Joe had a constant stream of people in and out of his room for the next ninety minutes. First was the upper limb specialist, who advised him he would need surgery on his hand. The knife had cut through the flexor tendon of his little finger. It could have been worse but even so it would mean six weeks in a hand splint, and surgery had been scheduled for her afternoon list today.

The surgeon had been followed by the police, who wanted a statement from him, but he had no good answer for them about why he'd acted as he had. He'd *reacted*. That was the best explanation he had. He'd reacted without thinking.

Although not totally without thought, but his only consideration had been for Kitty. He'd been taught to assess the danger before diving in but there hadn't been time for that. He'd seen Kitty lying on the floor and reacted, ignoring all his training. His only thought had been Kitty's safety, he hadn't considered his own at all.

Despite the fact that Joe hadn't exactly followed protocols, the police also wanted to know if he would like to press charges. But unless pressing charges meant Kitty's assailant would be forced to undergo rehab Joe didn't see the point, and he didn't want to spend any longer than necessary on filing paperwork. He wanted everyone to get out of his room—unless they were bringing him news of Kitty.

But Paula went one better than news. Five minutes after the police had left she wheeled Kitty into his room.

His heart missed a beat when he saw her in a wheelchair. She had dark circles under her eyes but she was smiling. Maybe things weren't as bad as he'd feared. 'Kitty! Are you OK?'

She nodded slowly. 'I have a concussion, a headache, a bit of dizziness and a few bruises, but otherwise I'm fine,' she said, as Paula put the brakes on the wheelchair and told them she'd be back in ten minutes.

'And the baby?'

'Is fine too,' Kitty said, as she stood and took the two steps to Joe's bedside. She bent over and kissed his cheek. 'I'm doing better than you by the looks of things.'

'I'm OK.' He was much better now that he'd seen her with his own two eyes.

'Lisa said you got stabbed.'

'Slashed, more precisely.' He held up his right hand, downplaying his injuries. 'A cut to my hand and one to my stomach.'

'Lisa also said you saved my life.'

'That's a definite over-exaggeration.'

Kitty wasn't so sure. She preferred to believe Lisa's version of events. The version where Joe had rushed to her side like a knight in shining armour. No one had ever done that for her before. It sounded very romantic but she knew she'd just embarrass him if she made a big deal out of it. It *was* a big deal to her. 'Thank you anyway,' she said, before kissing his cheek again. 'How long will you be in here for?' she asked as she sat carefully on the edge of his bed.

'Hopefully only until tomorrow. I'm having surgery on my hand this afternoon.'

'Surgery?'

'I have to have a tendon repaired, which means six weeks in a splint, but I shouldn't need long in hospital.'

'Does that mean six weeks off work?' Kitty asked. She knew he'd go mad from boredom if he was out of action for that long.

'I'm sure there will be office work or something I can do,' he said. 'Paramedics are always getting injured on the job, there's a constant rotation through the office of ambos on light duties or returning from extended time off. I'm sure they'll find me something. Otherwise I'll go around to Cam and Jess's and help paint the nursery.'

'Left-handed?'

'Sure.'

She smiled. 'Jess won't let you anywhere near her nursery. She's been planning it for ever.' Jess was an interior designer and Kitty knew that her baby's nursery would be the most important project her sister had ever tackled. She had already spent hours obsessing over paint colours, fabrics and furniture to make sure it was perfect. 'You're going to be sidelined for a while, though, aren't you? Showering and dressing will be difficult, let alone cooking.' She'd been a nurse for long enough to know the difficulties Joe would face, being right-handed *and* living alone. 'You might have to get Victoria to give you a hand when you're discharged.'

'Victoria?'

'Yes, haven't the two of you got a thing going on?'

'We hooked up a couple of times if that's what you mean but I wouldn't say we had a thing. I've told her it can't be anything serious and I certainly won't be asking her to help me out.'

Joe *never* had anything serious going on with his women, Kitty knew that. He went through them faster than Kitty could blink but suddenly her day didn't seem quite so dismal.

'What will you do?'

'No idea,' he replied. 'I'll figure something out.'

'I can help if you'd like?'

'What with? I'm not letting you do all the heavy lifting when you're seven months pregnant.'

'Why not? It won't be hard, in fact, it'll be easier than what I have to cope with at work. No aggressive drugged-out patients, for a start. And I won't be allowed back to work until my symptoms have all settled. We can keep each other company while we recover,' she said, as Paula returned to take her back to her room. 'Think about it. I'll come back and see you later after your surgery. You can tell me your answer then.'

'When I'm groggy from the anaesthetic and not thinking straight?'

'Something like that,' she said with a smile, as she kissed him on the cheek and sat back in the wheelchair. 'But don't think this discussion is over.'

* * *

Jess got up again to fetch another drink from the water cooler in the corner of the oncologist's waiting room. Cam had offered to fetch it for her as her coughing fit showed no signs of abating, but his wife seemed to be having trouble sitting still.

Cam knew she was on edge. She always went into these appointments expecting the worst, and he always sat there feeling useless and wishing there was something he could do to fix everything. And today was worse than usual due to the added stress over Kitty and the baby after yesterday's assault.

'I'm sure it's going to be fine,' he said, trying to reassure her while knowing that was near impossible. For two years after she'd undergone the hysterectomy for uterine cancer Jess had been having follow-up reviews every three months, but these were now being stretched out to every six months and as far as Cam could work out that was a positive sign. Everything had been fine six months ago, and in his mind there was no reason to think anything would be different this time. But he knew that Jess's mind worked differently from his. 'We'll have the check-up, and then we can go and collect Kitty.'

He was hoping distraction would work as a technique. Kitty was being discharged today and she was waiting for Cam and Jess to collect her after this appointment. Cam hoped that if Jess was thinking about Kitty while they waited to see the specialist perhaps she wouldn't dwell on her own situation. Waiting was always the worst part. The sooner Jess got in to see the doctor the sooner they'd hear good news and the sooner things would be back to normal.

He held her hand and gave it a squeeze. He waited for her to look at him and then he smiled. She smiled back but he could see the effort it cost her and his heart ached. He wished he could relieve all her worries. He loved her and he hated to see her worried or stressed, and he hated feeling so helpless. Not for the first time he wished that he had been the one who had cancer. He would much prefer to have been the one to suffer rather than watching Jess suffer. Her diagnosis had taken a toll on both of them. He didn't imagine that the same wouldn't have been true in the reverse situation but he'd still rather be the one suffering the physical and emotional pain if it meant sparing Jess that burden.

'Jess?' Dr Tennant called them into the consulting room just as Jess started coughing again. She drained the cup of water and refilled it before entering the room as Cam held the door for her. 'How are you feeling?' the oncologist asked as they sat down.

'Tired,' Jess replied, and Cam felt a flicker of concern. Jess hadn't mentioned that to him. 'I've been decorating a nursery,' she continued, and Cam saw that she was smiling and he relaxed. Her fatigue was simply a result of physical activity. 'The surrogacy worked,' Jess said. She'd talked of nothing else at the last oncology appointment. 'We're expecting a baby. My sister is the surrogate.'

'Congratulations! How far along is she?'

'Twenty-eight weeks,' Jess said, before another bout of coughing caught up with her.

Dr Tennant was watching Jess closely and Cam saw her make a note in Jess's file.

'Is that the only reason you're tired?' she queried.

Jess shrugged. 'I'm not sleeping that well. This cough is bugging me.'

Cam's concern spiked again. He knew

Jess's cough woke her during the night—it woke them both—but he'd thought she always managed to get back to sleep.

'How long have you had it?'

'I'm not sure. A few weeks?' Jess said, as she looked at Cam for confirmation.

He nodded but then stopped to think. 'Maybe longer,' he suggested. He'd got used to it, they both had, and he couldn't really remember exactly when it had started. With all the excitement over the pregnancy they'd probably both ignored it but the expression on the doctor's face was bothering him. They'd ignored the cough but the doctor looked like she didn't think it was nothing.

'Hop on the scales for me,' Dr Tennant instructed.

'You've lost weight,' she said, as Jess got off the scales and slipped her shoes back on. And Cam felt the first real flicker of alarm building in his chest.

CHAPTER SIX

JESS KNEW SHE'D lost weight recently. She'd tried to increase her portion sizes to counteract it but her appetite hadn't been great and she rarely finished a meal.

'Any other changes?' the doctor continued. 'Headaches? Chest pain? Unusual bleeding? Shortness of breath?'

'Headaches,' she admitted.

'Headaches?' Cam repeated. It was no wonder he sounded surprised. She hadn't said anything to him about the headaches, presumably because she hadn't wanted him to worry.

'Just a few,' she said, trying to wipe out the worry in Cam's eyes, although if she was honest it was more like one, constant, dull headache in the background of her life, which occasionally got worse before settling again.

Dr Tennant popped a stethoscope into

her ears and listened to Jess's chest. 'Deep breaths,' she instructed. 'No temperature?' she queried as she packed the stethoscope away.

Jess shook her head.

'Is your cough productive?'

Jess nodded.

'OK. I'd like to send off a sputum sample and I'm also going to send you for a CT scan of your chest.'

'What are you looking for?'

'What do you think it is?' Jess and Cam spoke in unison. Jess was worried now and she slipped her hand into Cam's, needing the security of his touch, even though it wasn't going to affect the oncologist's answer.

'I'm not going to hazard a guess without more information. We'll run some tests and then I'll discuss the results with you when I get them.'

She drew some blood and took a sputum sample before printing out a referral for the CT scan. Jess's hand was shaking as she took the piece of paper.

Cam kept hold of her hand as they left the doctor's office. Jess didn't think she would have made it out of there without his support.

'Do you want to grab something to eat before we collect Kitty?' Cam asked.

Jess shook her head. 'No, I'm not hungry. And please don't say anything to Kitty about the tests,' she said as they took the lift to Kitty's floor. 'She's still recovering from the attack and I don't want her to worry about something that will hopefully be nothing.'

But that didn't stop her palms from sweating and her heart from racing. She tried to keep calm, tried to keep her composure. She didn't want to upset Cam or Kitty, but she was worried. She'd been worried for a while but had been trying to ignore her symptoms by focussing on Kitty's pregnancy, on their baby, but the truth was she *hadn't* been feeling well and had been pretending everything was fine. That was why she'd been edgier than normal today—she knew Cam had noticed—because she'd been expecting bad news. She hadn't got it yet but she certainly hadn't been reassured by anything the oncologist had said. Dr Tennant hadn't needed to spell it out for her. She knew she was on borrowed time.

Kitty stepped out of Cam's car as he pulled to a stop in front of Joe's building. She had spent one night at her sister's house after she'd been discharged from hospital but now she had convinced Joe to let her nurse him. She hovered over him as he gingerly unfolded himself from the back seat. The hospital was only a ten-minute drive from his house but the whole process of discharge appeared to have taken its toll. Kitty could see the little tell-tale lines of pain gathering at the corners of his mouth. She needed to get him upstairs and get some painkillers into him.

She was pleased he had accepted her offer of help. She was pleased, too, that things were over between him and Victoria, although she didn't want to think about the sort of friend that made her—taking pleasure in the fact that Joe had just ended a relationship. But she didn't feel too mean-spirited. Their break-up suited her—now she could have him to herself.

Cam carried Kitty's small overnight bag up the stairs to Joe's third-floor flat as Kitty continued to hover anxiously over Joe. He held his left hand against his stomach, over his wound, and took the stairs slowly but steadily.

'Are you sure you don't want to come and

stay at our place, Joe?' Cam asked when they reached his door. 'We don't have any stairs.'

'I appreciate the offer, mate, but after two nights in hospital I'm really looking forward to being in my own bed.'

'Fair enough, but the offer stands. You can take it up at any time if you change your mind.'

'Is Jess OK with me staying here with Joe for a little while?' Kitty asked as they went inside. 'She doesn't feel like I'm abandoning her?'

Cam hesitated before answering and Kitty held her breath. She hoped she wasn't upsetting her sister by opting to look after Joe, but she really wanted to do this.

'She'll miss you,' Cam replied eventually, 'but she understands. Just don't make it permanent, at least not while you're pregnant. She feels more connected to the pregnancy if you're under our roof.'

'I know. I'll be back before you know it. Tell her it won't be for ever,' Kitty said. Nothing in her life seemed to last for ever, so why would this living situation be any different?

'Where do you want me to put your bag?' Cam asked.

'Put it in my room,' Joe replied.

'Leave it out here,' Kitty said at the same time. 'I'll sleep on the couch.'

'You're kidding, aren't you?' Joe remarked.

'Why not? I did before,' Kitty replied.

'This is different now. You're pregnant.'

'All right, I'll leave you to sort that out. I'm going to get home to Jess,' Cam said as he backed out of the flat.

'Thanks for the lift, Cam,' Kitty said. 'Tell Jess I'll pop over to see her tomorrow.'

Cam looked as if he was about to say something in response and Kitty waited, but he seemed to change his mind and just nodded and turned away. Kitty shrugged her shoulders as he closed the door, wondering if she'd imagined the look in his eyes—almost as though he was debating whether or not to say more. He knew where to find her, she supposed, as she turned back to continue her conversation with Joe.

'I think, with your injuries, your bed is the best place for you. You even told Cam you were looking forward to being back in it.'

'And I am. But I thought we'd share.'

'Share?'

'Yeah. It's a king-size, there's plenty of room for both of us.'

Maybe, Kitty thought, *but that was before I started thinking about kissing you. Before my pregnancy hormones made me think about sex twenty-four seven. Before I wanted to tear your clothes off...*

For a moment she wondered how this was going to work. She couldn't imagine sleeping peacefully next to him, not with her rampaging hormones. But he *was* injured—that should dampen his libido—and he hadn't shown any signs of wanting to get down and dirty with her anyway, so she'd just have to rein her hormones in and keep her hands to herself. It could be a long six weeks. But Joe wasn't waiting for her to mentally process the situation. He was still talking.

'...to help.'

'Sorry, what did you say?'

'I appreciate you offering to help me out for the next few weeks but I'm only accepting on the condition that you sleep in my bed. I meant it when I said I wasn't going to let you take the couch. If I thought I'd get any sleep on the sofa *I'd* take it, but there's room for us both in the bed. Although if you think it will be a problem, I can organise a home nurse to come in once a day to give me a hand.'

The new, crazily hormonal, pregnant Kitty knew it would test her reserves but she *had* offered to help. She'd have to summon up the old Kitty and block out all the crazy day-dreams and fantasies.

'Of course we'll manage,' she said as she settled Joe on the couch and busied herself with some housework. She put fresh sheets on the bed and put a load of dirty sheets into the washing machine. She put the kettle on and prepared a simple dinner—omelettes and salad—and pretended everything was completely normal.

Joe was back on the couch after dinner but Kitty's head was aching. Trying to keep busy and avoid sitting down with Joe had its downsides. She'd overdone it when she should have been resting too, and now she was paying the price. It was time for some paracetamol and bed.

She yawned and stretched. 'I think I might call it a night. Will you be able to get yourself undressed if I go to bed now?'

'I'll be fine,' he said. He was wearing tracksuit pants and a T-shirt that he could pull over his head with one hand. They weren't difficult clothes to get out of. In fact, perhaps it wouldn't be a bad idea if he *didn't* get undressed.

Kitty changed into an oversized T-shirt and swallowed a couple of painkillers. If she'd imagined she and Joe would be sharing a bed she would have packed a pair of pyjama bottoms but she didn't currently have any that fitted comfortably. Her expanding waistline made everything too tight. She climbed into bed after first working out what side Joe slept on—there was a charging dock for his phone and a couple of books on the left-hand side of the bed, so Kitty opted for the right side— and pulled the covers up to disguise the fact that she was almost naked.

She woke to find herself spooning in Joe's arms. His left arm was draped across her, resting on her stomach. He was warm and she was comfortable and she couldn't see the harm in lying there for a few moments while she enjoyed the feel of him. She imagined she could feel his heart beating against her back. She wondered if he was awake. She listened to the sound of his breathing, trying to judge.

She was tempted to roll over. Tempted to see what he was wearing.

She could feel his breath on her neck and his stubble was rough on her skin. She liked the feel of it. She was aware of everything. She could even feel each of his fingertips through her shirt where they rested against her belly. It felt good to be lying in his arms. Too good.

She wondered what would happen if she rolled over. They would be lying inches apart. Less.

What would happen? Would he kiss her? Would he back away if she kissed him?

The baby moved, interrupting her train of thought and bringing her back to reality with a sharp and carefully placed kick. She felt the baby push against her belly. Against Joe's hand.

'Was that the baby?'

He was awake.

Suddenly she was more conscious of the position they were in. It had felt comfortable when she'd thought he was asleep, but now she was aware of how intimate it actually was. But it was too late to worry about that now.

She could feel the baby's leg pushing sideways, distending her belly. What would the old Kitty have done in this situation? She summoned up those memories of a simpler time and interlaced her fingers with Joe's. She moved his hand slightly, holding it over the baby's foot. 'She's doing her morning exercises,' she told him.

Joe could hear the smile in Kitty's voice. He hadn't meant to wake in this position but he wasn't complaining. As always, she fitted just perfectly into his embrace, even if this position was far from their usual.

He'd been awake for several minutes, lying quietly, enjoying the feeling of having Kitty in his arms, trying not to wake her. He had no idea if he'd ever get this chance again.

She smelt fantastic. He closed his eyes and breathed in her familiar vanilla scent. She smelt like she felt—warm and soft and sweet. He wanted to bury himself in her. Inhale her, breathe her in, not let her go.

He'd expected her to wake and move out of his arms immediately. He'd expected her to be flustered, embarrassed, affronted, all manner of things, but he hadn't expected this. This intimacy, this easiness.

Her hips were pressed in against him. Or

he was pressed against her. He could feel his erection nestled in the cleft in her buttocks, but as far as he could tell Kitty hadn't noticed. Perhaps she was too distracted by the baby's movements. It was incredible to think that Kitty would be having this experience several times a day. That she had a tiny human growing inside her.

Even though he was doing his best to be supportive, he still wasn't thrilled about the fears for the future that this pregnancy brought up, but he had to admit he was grateful to the baby right now. If it hadn't started moving he suspected Kitty would have been up and out of bed before she'd even woken properly once she realised the position they were in, but half-asleep and still relaxed, she seemed happy to lie there.

He could feel her body heat radiating through her shirt and into his hand and against his chest. She was like a little hot-water bottle. He knew the pregnancy was raising her body temperature. His was raised too, and he knew what was causing that. Heat and desire surged through him.

Waking in this position felt extremely intimate. Intimate and sensual. It made him think about waking like this every morning and how that would feel. He never usually thought into the future like that. He lived in the moment as far as intimacy was concerned, never imagining that his relationships could develop into something permanent. He knew that was one of his major character flaws: an inability to commit.

Lord knew, neither of his parents seemed to be able to manage it. Why would he be any different? But for the first time ever, the idea of waking up every day with a woman in his bed, in his arms, didn't frighten the life out of him.

He knew the reason was because of the woman.

This wasn't about him and his failings—Kitty made him want to try to be a better man. He wanted to try to be the man she needed.

He wondered if that was even possible for him. Could he be that man? What would Kitty think? Could he risk finding out? Should he take a chance?

But before he had time to answer his own question, Kitty had moved away from him.

'Ouch! The baby just kicked my bladder,' she said as she pushed back the covers and climbed out of bed. Cool morning air rushed under the sheets. Kitty had taken her warmth, and his chance, with her, leaving him with a missed opportunity and an ache in his groin.

She disappeared into the bathroom without a backward glance and he wondered if the baby was really causing problems or if Kitty had just needed an excuse to get out of bed.

Kitty wished she'd been brave enough to take a chance. To roll over when she'd wanted to, before the baby's mistimed kick had connected with her bladder and given her no choice but to get out of bed.

Perhaps it was just as well, she thought as she closed the bathroom door. She didn't think she could stand being rejected again. She felt as though she'd only just recovered her equilibrium after their almost-kiss.

She needed time to cool down, to collect her thoughts. She turned on the taps in the shower and stepped under the spray. She imagined she could still feel the imprint of Joe's arm around her, of his hand resting on her belly, before the water washed it away.

She ran her soapy hands over her breasts, imagining how it would feel to have Joe touch her. To have Joe's fingers on her breast, his tongue on her nipple...

God, she was aroused. Her hormones were driving her crazy.

She breathed out, battling to get herself under control. Her imagination wasn't helping.

Perhaps she'd have to rethink her offer to stay and help him. She'd been mad to think she could handle it. But there was no getting out of it this morning. She'd have to manage for at least one day. She needed to get herself together and work out how to control her impulses before they got her into trouble.

She rested her hands on the cool tiles on the wall and let the water run down between her shoulder blades while she forced her mind to go blank.

She stepped out of the shower, dried herself and pulled her T-shirt back over her head. She had nothing else to put on and didn't think it was wise to come out of the bathroom wrapped only in a towel. She stepped into her underwear. Her clothing wasn't much of a defence against her rampaging desire, but it was all she had.

Joe hadn't moved. He was still lying in bed when she returned from the bathroom. His chest was bare, tanned and smooth. Her pulse quickened and heat flushed her cheeks.

Her gaze flicked down before she could stop herself, following the line of his sternum, down the centre of his abdominals before it stopped at the bed sheet that was pulled up to his hips. She still didn't know if he was naked under the sheet. Surely he couldn't be. He wouldn't have come to bed wearing nothing. More's the pity.

But wondering about Joe's state of undress was not the way to get herself under control. She needed something to keep her mind occupied.

'Do you want to shower?' she asked quickly. 'I'll waterproof your arm for you if you like.'

'Sounds good,' he said as he rolled out of bed. His abdominal muscles rippled as he lifted his head, and Kitty held her breath as the sheet fell away and he swung his legs out of bed to stand up.

Kitty's eyes dropped lower. She couldn't help herself.

He was wearing boxer shorts.

Her disappointment was abated a little by the impressive bulge in his shorts.

She swallowed uncertainly and took a step back. Not that she was standing too close, but it was instinctive to try to put some space between them. Some physical distance. His semi-nakedness was making her nervous. She wasn't sure exactly how she was going to keep her hormones in check and fight the attraction if they were going to be in such close proximity for the next few weeks.

She got busy fetching a plastic bag and tape to protect the splint on his arm from the shower spray. She really should be protecting *herself*. She couldn't afford to cross the line. Joe's friendship was far too important.

She sat next to him on the bed. So much for keeping her distance—she could feel the heat radiating off him, and she could smell the sleepiness of his body. It was a warm, familiar scent.

His bare knees brushed against hers as she turned to him and pulled the plastic bag over his splint. They'd sat like this plenty of times before, but never in a bedroom. It had never felt this intimate before. She covered his arm carefully, her fingers light on his skin as if she was afraid to touch him, afraid of what that might lead to, and secured it with the tape.

'Can you manage everything else?' she asked, hoping he would say no but half-wishing he'd say yes. Wishing he'd make the first move, take the first step and take the decision away from her. If he made a move she knew she wouldn't resist. She wouldn't have the willpower.

'I can.' He was watching her carefully, his blue eyes dark, making her breath catch in her throat. Was that sleep or desire turning his eyes indigo?

She knew she should get dressed while Joe was in the shower but she couldn't seem to make her legs move. They were heavy and uncooperative, so she stayed sitting on the bed.

'Kitty? Can you give me a hand?' She heard the shower stop running and heard him call to her.

She went into the bathroom.

Joe had managed to remove the plastic bag that had protected the splint from his arm and was now, very definitely, completely naked. Kitty could feel her blood pounding in her veins. She wasn't sure what she'd expected to find, but she hadn't prepared herself for this. She felt like she knew him so well yet she'd never seen him completely naked before.

Fortunately, or perhaps unfortunately— she wasn't certain yet—he had his back to her. His shoulders were broad and tanned and she could see the outline of his trapezius muscles above his shoulder blades and the ridge of muscle running down either side of his spine. She wanted desperately to run her fingers along his spine, to trace the length of his body, but she had to be content to savour him with her eyes instead. Her gaze trailed down to the cleft between his buttocks. His backside was firm, muscular, nicely rounded. Two perfect globes, slightly paler than the rest of his skin but not much. His buttocks looked smooth and cool, like marble, and her fingers itched to run over his skin, to feel it under her palm.

He was holding a towel in his left hand, obviously unable to wrap it around himself with only one hand. She reached for the towel, resisting the urge to reach for him, and took it from his fingers. From behind she reached around him, wrapping the towel around his waist and tucking one end into the other over his left hip. It seemed such a pity to cover up the view. But then he turned around. Now she was face to face with his naked chest. This she'd seen before, many times, but somehow today it seemed far more intimidating.

She'd rested her head against that same chest on plenty of occasions. She couldn't count the number of times he'd hugged her, but she couldn't recall him ever hugging her shirtless. She didn't think she'd ever been this close to his bare chest before and she was copping an eyeful—a very attractive eyeful. His chest was still damp and little droplets of moisture glistened on his skin and caught in the fine hair that ran down between the ridge of his abdominals.

The air around them felt positively charged, making it difficult to breathe. Maybe it was just the steaminess of the bathroom. The hot, humid air was heavy and it was an effort to breathe it in. She was feeling a little light-headed. She needed to get him dry and dressed and get out of there.

She stepped back and her eyes dropped lower, down to where the trail of hair disappeared beneath the towel. Her eyes caught on the waterproof dressing above his right hip. The dressing that covered the knife wound. The wound he'd got protecting her. She wondered if he thought it was worth it.

'I would,' he said.

She lifted her eyes and met his gaze. His blue eyes were dark, his gaze unwavering.

'Would what?' she asked.

'I would do it again. To protect you.' His voice was deep, quiet, intense and honest, and his words sent a shiver of anticipation and excitement through her.

She dropped her gaze again, needing to break the spell, and reached out and traced the edges of the dressing with her fingers. His skin was warm. That surprised her. She'd expected it to be cool by now. The warmth of his skin made her fingers feel icy in contrast, and she could see little goose-bumps rising on his stomach, heard him catch his breath.

'Sorry, are my hands cold?'

'No.' His voice was husky now and his eyes an even more intense blue.

Her hand stilled as she looked up at him.

Everything about him looked hard and intense—his body, his gaze, his intentions, his need, his desire—and Kitty's heart pounded in her chest. Her breath caught again in her throat.

She didn't know what she should do. Should she reach for him? Tell him how she was feeling? She was so unsure, and her uncertainty made her take a step back just as he stepped forward.

He reached for her. She felt his fingers under her chin and now it was *her* skin that tingled and broke out in tiny goose-bumps.

He whispered her name as he tipped her head up and Kitty closed her eyes, waiting for the kiss she knew was coming this time.

His lips met hers, warm and soft, but his intentions were clear, spelt out in his touch as he pressed his lips against hers. Kitty opened her mouth, desperate to taste him, to feel him, to experience him. She breathed out a sigh as he wrapped his left arm around her, holding her to him. Her hands wound around the back of his neck. His hair was damp—she probably needed to get him dry, but she had other things on her mind.

She could feel his erection, separated from

her only by the towel and her underwear. He was hard and long and now all she could think about was how he would feel inside her. She could feel the dampness between her thighs as she imagined him thrusting into her. Uniting them in a way they'd never shared before. Her knees wobbled and she clung to him. In another moment there would be no turning back.

That was good—she didn't *want* to turn back—but he was injured and she didn't want to be the one responsible for pulling his stitches out, opening his wounds.

'Careful,' she whispered. 'You're injured, remember?'

His left hand moved further down her back, cupping her bottom, pulling her hips in hard against him. 'I'm fine,' he replied.

She ran one hand down his chest. She had to agree, he felt pretty fine. His chest was dry now—the water had soaked into her T-shirt, making it cling to her skin. Now that her clothes were damp and she wasn't pressed against his chest, soaking up his warmth, she felt cool. Her nipples jutted against the shirt and as she saw Joe run his gaze over her breasts she felt her nipples tighten in response.

She watched his chest rise as he inhaled. He moved his left arm, bringing his hand to her chest and running his thumb over one nipple, caressing it through the fabric.

Kitty thought she might melt on the spot as a burst of heat raced through her, flaring from her breasts to her groin.

'Oh, God, Joe,' she said as she clung to him, and she could hear the desire and need in her voice.

'Are you sure about this?'

'I've never been surer about anything,' she said, as she took his hand and led him out of the bathroom.

He caught her at the edge of the bed and turned her to face him. He pulled the towel from his hips and stood in front of her gloriously, superbly naked. Kitty feasted her eyes on him. She took in his broad shoulders, the dark circles of his nipples, the line of dark hair running down from his navel, leading her eyes down to where his erection jutted proudly out from his hips.

He ran his hand around the back of her

neck, spanning her spine with his fingers, holding her still as he kissed her neck. Kitty tipped her head back, exposing the soft, tender, sensitive skin of her throat.

He lifted the hem of her T-shirt, keeping her close, before trying to tug the shirt up and off, but it was an impossible task with only one hand. Kitty crossed her arms and whipped the shirt over her head.

'You are beautiful,' he murmured before he bent his head and took one breast in his mouth. Kitty thought she might explode as he sucked her nipple. He ran his hand over her swollen belly and down between her thighs, seeking her warmth, sliding into her wetness.

Joe went to sit down on the edge of the bed and Kitty moved with him, stepping out of her underwear as she did. She stood with her legs apart, straddling his knees, desperate to maintain contact, and granted him access to her innermost secrets.

Her legs buckled as his mouth suckled at her breast again while he reached between her legs, his thumb moving in a tight circle. She rested her hands on his shoulders, supporting her weight. Her legs certainly weren't capable of holding her up as he worked his magic with his fingers. If he could reduce her to a quivering mess with his left hand, what would he be able to do once his right hand was fully functioning again?

She closed her eyes as stars burst behind her eyelids and sparks shot through her groin. She was panting now, unable to take deep breaths as her body was focussed on other sensations. She was close to a climax, she could feel it building, taking control, but she didn't want it like this.

She opened her eyes. 'Wait.'

'What's wrong?' His hand stilled and she could see in his eyes that he was expecting her to call it quits. There was no way she was doing that—she didn't think she could stop now even if she wanted to.

'Nothing,' she said, 'but I want to feel you inside me.'

He smiled, relief and desire reflected in his eyes now. 'You'll have to go on top.'

She had no problem with that. In reply she pushed him gently backwards until he was lying on the bed.

'There are condoms in the drawer,' he told her.

She was about to remind him that she was

pregnant and that she didn't need protection but then she thought about all the other reasons to practise safe sex. She supposed she should be grateful that he was being responsible, but she didn't want to think about *why* he had condoms in his bedside drawer. She didn't want to think about all the other women he might have slept with in this bed. It was her turn now and she didn't want to waste a second thinking about anything other than Joe and the pleasure they were about to share.

She reached into the drawer and removed one little packet. She knelt over him and wrapped her hand firmly around his shaft. She slid her hand up and down his length and felt him throb beneath her fingers, felt him tremor under her touch. She watched as he closed his eyes and relaxed on the bed, breathing in and out, slow and deep.

'Kitty, please,' he begged, his voice ragged and breathless.

Her hand slowed but she maintained contact as she tore open the packet with her teeth and sheathed his erection. It was, she imagined, another impossible task to accomplish one-handed. His eyes were open now and he watched her as she lifted herself onto her knees and slowly lowered herself down onto him. She took her time, savouring the moment when they were finally, blissfully joined together.

She placed her hands on either side of his head, supporting her weight as she bent over him. He lifted his head and took her breast into his mouth as she rode him. Their hips moved in perfect harmony, his thrusts keeping time to her rhythm, as if they'd done this dance a hundred times before. His fingers were between her legs, circling the swollen nub that nestled there. Kitty arched her back and spread her legs wider, taking him deeper, wanting all of him, every last piece as waves of pleasure overwhelmed her.

'Now, Joe, now!'

She felt him join her in pleasure and then release, their years of friendship shifting and changing and culminating into something far more powerful, far more thrilling than anything she had experienced before.

She lay beside him, utterly spent, resting her head on his chest, and listened to his breathing as she lay cocooned in his arms. She felt completely relaxed and content, and the feeling surprised her. She had thought there might be some awkwardness but instead she felt like she belonged there. It was a strange but wonderful sensation.

CHAPTER SEVEN

KITTY EMBRACED JESS as she opened the door. She felt thin, but Kitty didn't think anything of it. Jess had always been slim, especially since the chemo, and now her slightness felt even more apparent when contrasted with Kitty's changing shape as she went further into her third trimester of the pregnancy.

'How are you feeling?' Jess asked.

'Exhausted,' Kitty replied as she followed Jess into the house.

'You should have called. You could have come over later.'

She realised Jess thought her tiredness was due to the concussion. Should she tell her it was because she'd spent the better part of the last two hours in bed with Joe, exercising muscles she almost hadn't remembered having?

'No, no, it's fine. I wanted to see you.'

She stuck her head into the baby's nursery, eager to see what Jess had been up to for the past few days. She hadn't thought to look at it yesterday when her head had still been woozy from the concussion and she was surprised to find it almost finished. The bottom half of the walls had been papered in a gorgeous pale green-and-white-striped wallpaper that Kitty hadn't seen before, and mobiles hung from the ceiling above the newly assembled change table and cot. Tucked into one corner in front of a small bookcase and reading lamp was an inviting armchair upholstered in a pale apple green.

'Wow, you've been busy.'

'I had some time on my hands,' Jess said. 'I'm keen to get it finished. It was strange being in the house without you. And without the baby. Working on the nursery made me feel connected to you both, although I can't take credit for much more than the design choices and dressing the cot. I'm keen to meet my baby and I sort of feel that if I get the nursery ready, maybe it will hurry things up. At least *I* feel ready.'

'Don't be in too much of a hurry, I've got a while to go yet!' Kitty wasn't ready for the pregnancy to end yet. The baby wasn't due for another eleven weeks or so, and she wasn't quite ready to give the baby up.

'I know,' Jess replied. 'But I needed something to keep me busy. How is everything going in there?' She asked as she put her hand on Kitty's belly. Kitty was getting used to people touching her stomach without asking. Everyone seemed to think of it as separate from her and didn't seem to think they needed permission. But in this case Kitty didn't mind. Jess *definitely* didn't need permission. After all, the baby was hers.

'Are you positive you're fine after the incident? Both of you?'

Kitty nodded. 'I'm sure. I've got a few bruises and a dull headache still, but the baby is perfectly fine.'

'Your shape has changed,' Jess said as she took her hand off Kitty's tummy. 'That seems to have happened quickly.'

Kitty saw a flash of something on her sister's face but she didn't have time to work out what it was. Sadness? Regret? Anxiety? Distress?

Kitty remembered Cam's expression of the day before. The similarities between his expression and Jess's now didn't go unnoticed. Maybe staying at Joe's wasn't the right thing to do. She knew Jess wanted—needed—to feel connected to the pregnancy. Maybe she should be here? But Joe needed her too. Kitty was torn. She wasn't used to having so many people relying on her.

'Is everything OK?' she asked. 'Do you want me to move back in? Joe can organise for a home nurse,' she offered but hoped, at the same time, that Jess would refuse her suggestion. How could she tell who needed her more? It made her concussed brain hurt even more just thinking about what to do.

'No, don't be silly,' Jess said as she ushered Kitty out of the room. She was back to her usual no-nonsense organised self as she hustled to the kitchen and flicked on the kettle, and Kitty breathed a sigh of relief as she shrugged off the incident. Perhaps she'd imagined Jess's look of distress. She chose to ignore it for the moment. It was easier to pretend it hadn't happened than to think about having to make a choice. If she had to choose between Joe and Jess she wasn't sure what she'd do at the moment. They were both important to her. They were *the* most important people in her world. The two of them and the baby.

'So, how is Joe?' Jess asked as she poured boiling water into two mugs and dropped bags of green tea into the liquid before letting it steep.

Kitty realised she wanted to tell Jess about what had happened. She was too excited to keep it to herself. She'd finally had sex with Joe, made love to him, and it was every bit as good as she'd been imagining over the past few weeks. Better, even.

'Why are you smiling like that? What's happened?'

Kitty hadn't realised she was smiling.

'I had sex with Joe,' she admitted.

'What! Oh, my God!' Jess dropped the packet of biscuits she was opening but appeared to gather her wits as she picked up the fallen cookies. She was grinning when she looked back up at Kitty. 'It's about time. How was it? I hope it was brilliant.'

'What do you mean, "It's about time"?'

'Cam and I have been hoping the two of you would get together, but we were beginning to think it would never happen.'

'You've talked about this?'

'Of course,' Jess said as she put the untainted biscuits on a plate on the kitchen table. 'We love Joe. The two of you would be perfect together, but we were worried that you were destined to be friends and only friends for ever.'

Kitty *was* worried that she might have ruined their friendship. 'Do you think we can have sex and still be friends?'

'Of course. Cam and I are friends.'

'You're friends *now* but you weren't friends before you started dating.'

'That's true. But you and Joe have so much history. You don't have to worry about all the getting-to-know-you stuff. You already know you like him. Starting from friends is no problem. Not unless you end up making it one.'

Kitty knew Jess was speaking from experience. She knew what Kitty was like. She knew her tendencies. How she overthought *everything* and always feared the worst. The trouble was, the worst often happened.

'I don't want it to be a problem,' she said as Jess threw out the tea bags and passed her the cup. 'I'd like to think it could work, but what if it doesn't?'

'What would be worse,' Jess asked, 'giving it a go and finding out that it might be the best decision you ever made, or being too worried about what might go wrong that you miss out completely? From where I'm sitting it looks like you've chosen option one already.'

'You forgot option three.'

'Which is?'

'Being brave and then it ends in total disaster anyway.'

'Are you sorry you slept with him?'

How could she be sorry? It was the best sex she'd ever had.

Kitty shook her head. She didn't regret what they'd done but all the doubts were threatening to take the gloss off the experience.

'And he doesn't seem sorry either?' Jess asked.

Kitty shook her head again.

'And are you happy right now?'

She was going to say she wasn't sure, but she closed her eyes and she could see Joe's face. She could feel his hands on her body. His lips on her skin. It had felt right then and the memory felt right now. 'Yes.'

'Then I think you should relax. Don't overthink things, have some fun. So tell me—what was he like?' Jess was smiling.

Kitty sighed, still lost in her memories of last night. 'He was perfect.'

Joe was lying on the couch when Kitty let herself back in through his front door. He was barefoot and shirtless, and Kitty felt her libido kick into gear as she let her eyes roam over him.

She'd picked up a pizza on her way back and Joe sat up as she put the box on the coffee table. He grimaced as he moved despite the fact that he was holding his left hand over his abdominal wound, and Kitty remembered she hadn't got around to changing his dressing earlier.

'You came back.'

'Of course.' She frowned, not understanding. 'Why wouldn't I?'

'I was worried you might think we'd made a mistake this morning.'

That one simple sentence highlighted just how well he knew her. They'd been friends for so long that she sometimes felt he knew her better than she knew herself. She had been worrying about that. She'd worried that the painkillers had made them reckless, worried they might have ruined their friendship. She *always* thought of reasons why things wouldn't work, rather than thinking of all the reasons they could. 'Have we?'

'No.' He shook his head and pulled her down onto the couch beside him.

'You don't think we might ruin our friendship?'

'I'd like to think we can always be friends.'

'With benefits?' she asked.

Joe smiled at her, the familiar dimple appearing in his chin, and Kitty's stomach somersaulted.

'So I take it you enjoyed it?' he said as he reached out and ran his thumb down her cheek, tracing the line of her jaw, and trailed it across to her lips.

She could feel the heat radiating off him and her heart began to race. 'You know I did.'

His thumb moved back towards her cheek and he slid his fingers around behind her neck, cupping the back of her head. 'I promise we will always be friends. Things don't need to get awkward.'

She didn't think he could make that promise, but she also didn't think she could resist the silent overtures he was making. Sleeping with him once wasn't going to be enough for her.

He pulled her towards him and kissed her soundly, the pizza forgotten in its box on the table.

Kitty wondered if things were being changed for ever by their actions today, but she didn't care. It was a risk she was prepared to take, she thought as she gave herself up to him again.

'Hello, Jess. Cameron. How are you both?' Dr Tennant showed them to the chairs and waited until they both sat down before she started speaking. Jess noticed that the chairs were pushed very close together, as if the oncologist knew that Jess was going to need to be able to reach for Cam—as if she was going to need his support—and she knew what was coming next. 'I'm afraid I don't have good news for you.'

The room felt as though it was spinning, making Jess feel ill. She closed her eyes and reached out for Cam's hand. She felt his fingers wrap around hers and only then was she able to breathe again. She took a deep breath, opened her eyes and waited.

'The cancer has spread to your lungs, and there are some metastases in your brain as well.'

Jess fought back tears. She'd been expecting bad news, she'd felt it in her bones, which was ridiculous seeing as the doctor was telling her the cancer had spread to her lungs and brain, but she'd known something was wrong and she'd told herself she would be strong. For Cam's sake. But it was hard, almost impossible.

She wasn't strong.

'What do we do?' Cam asked.

'Treatment-wise our options are very limited.'

'What does that mean? Very limited?'

Cam was asking the questions, which was good as Jess couldn't speak. Fear of the future had frozen her tongue. But she didn't need to ask questions. She knew what it meant. She could feel it.

'It's difficult because of where it has spread to.'

'Can you get rid of it? Can you operate?'

The oncologist was shaking her head. 'It's

inoperable. The cancer is in both lungs and the brain. What it means is that treatment will focus on relieving Jess's symptoms, but we won't be able to cure it. I'm sorry. The best we can do is try to slow the spread.'

'With what?'

'Chemotherapy or radiotherapy. But any treatment will be palliative only.'

'Buying me time?' Jess found her voice and it caught in her throat as she spoke. 'Is that all you can do?'

The oncologist nodded. 'That's right. I'm very sorry.'

The doctor kept apologising but Jess barely heard her. All she heard was that the cancer had returned and she was on borrowed time.

'How long do I have?'

'With or without treatment?'

'Without.'

'Jess—' Cam started to speak but Jess stopped him.

'No, Cam, please, just listen. There is no cure, no fix and I really don't think I can go through chemo again. I need to know what my options are.' As an expectant mother, she would do whatever it took to ensure she got to hold her child, but she didn't want to be so sick from chemo that she couldn't enjoy the experience. Dr Tennant was telling her that treatment was palliative only. It wasn't going to give her any longer on this earth and therefore she needed to weigh up the positives and the negatives. 'My choice very much depends on what I can expect to gain from treatment. But it is *my* choice.'

She turned back to Dr Tennant. 'How long do I have?' she repeated.

'That's hard to say. The cancer is spreading rapidly. Weeks certainly. Months maybe.'

Weeks.

Kitty was thirty weeks pregnant. Jess couldn't let go now. 'You have to keep me alive for another ten weeks. I have to see my baby.' Her voice broke and she was shaking violently as tears spilled over her lashes onto her cheeks. 'I need to hold my baby. Please. Even just once. Tell me what I have to do.'

'Thoracic radiotherapy is your best option,' the oncologist suggested.

'Radiotherapy?' Cam queried. 'Not chemo?'

'Chemo is an option but not your best one,' the doctor spoke to Jess. 'The dose would be high, which means a higher level of toxicity. That would be OK if you were otherwise well, but you have other symptoms. In your case, radiotherapy will be more appropriate.'

'What about side effects?' Cam asked. Despite the fact that the treatment would be palliative and meant to give Jess relief from pain they both knew there were always side effects.

'The shortness of breath may get worse,' Dr Tennant said, 'and patients often have trouble swallowing, which can make eating difficult obviously. Also, if the radiation is given close to the stomach then you may experience nausea. But studies have shown that the level of comfort provided or the quality of life can be extended by about fifty per cent. I can't give you any guarantees but radiotherapy is your best chance of getting some relief.'

'So maybe some relief but not more time?' Jess said. This list didn't sound that different from the symptoms she was already experiencing. She wondered if it was worth it.

Dr Tennant shook her head. 'No. Time is something I can't give you.'

'I'll need to think about it,' Jess replied. 'Have I got time to do that?'

'Yes. Radiotherapy is not going to change

the outcome. All I can offer you is some relief. It's up to you when you need that.'

'What are we going to tell Kitty?' Cam asked as they left the hospital. He had his arm around his wife, supporting her.

'Nothing,' Jess replied. 'Not yet.' She was still shaking even though she wasn't cold, and she knew enough to recognise it as a manifestation of shock. She clung to Cam's hand, needing some of his strength. She wasn't strong enough to face this without him and she prayed he would support her decision about Kitty too.

'We can't keep this a secret.'

Jess realised that, but she needed time to process what she'd just heard and work out how to tell her sister. She had always appreciated the fact that Dr Tennant had never sugarcoated her opinion. She dealt in facts. But now the facts weren't what Jess wanted to hear. Now she realised exactly what the term *harsh reality* meant. Next she had to figure out how to deal with it. 'Please,' she begged. 'I need some time to work out what to say. You know how Kitty gets with bad news. She won't handle it well, and I'm worried about the baby.'

'The baby will be fine. Kitty is thirty weeks along,' Cam argued.

'I know but Kitty still needs to eat, rest and keep her strength up. I need her focussing on the baby, not on me. Just for a little bit longer. Please? And if we tell her now she'll want to move back in to be with me, and I think she should stay with Joe. Their relationship is only new. I don't want this news to jeopardise that for her. She's going to need Joe's support.'

'OK,' Cam agreed, 'but if you decide you're going to start radiotherapy, we're telling Kitty.'

Jess nodded. She'd agree for now to get her way and worry about everything else later.

Kitty put her key in the lock and let herself into Joe's place. She was starving, and something someone in the building was cooking smelt fantastic. She'd just had her first day back at work after the assault, and was looking forward to seeing Joe. They'd spent every night and most of every day together for the past two weeks and she'd missed him today when she'd gone back to work. It was good to be home.

Home.

This wasn't home. It was familiar and she'd spent plenty of time here, but it wasn't home. But it was starting to feel like it.

Could it be?

No. She shook her head as she closed the door. Joe wasn't the settling-down sort. She knew he didn't believe in serious commitment. He'd always said serious was not for him. She wondered, once again, if they'd made a mistake by sleeping together. Had they complicated their relationship? Was she risking their friendship for what could only be a dalliance? Joe wasn't going to make a long-term commitment. Not to her, not to anyone, and yet that was what she desired more than anything. There was no way she was going to survive if she ruined her relationship with Joe. He was too important. She wondered how they would get through this. Who would leave first?

It didn't bear thinking about.

She dumped her handbag on the chair by the front door as Joe stepped into the foyer. He was smiling at her and she promptly forgot all her concerns. His smile had always made her feel better and now it made her feel special.

'Hey, how was your day?' he asked as he greeted her with a kiss.

She could get used to this, she thought. 'Work was OK, but I missed you,' she replied honestly. Just because she knew they ultimately wanted different things was no reason to pretend she felt differently.

'I missed you too,' he said. His ran his left hand over the curve of her buttock as he nuzzled her neck, kissing the side of her throat.

She leant into him. 'What did you do all day?'

'I rang work to see when I can go back.'

Kitty straightened up and looked Joe in the eye. 'You remember the surgeon said six weeks minimum, don't you? It's only been just over two.'

'Yes, but I thought I'd be able to do some office work. There always seems to be someone on light duties, I figured it's my turn now. I'll go crazy stuck at home alone now that you're back at work.'

Kitty loved the idea that he was missing her, that he was lonely without her. Maybe this relationship *could* work. 'I start maternity leave in four weeks. I'll be around constantly then. You might get sick of me.'

'I don't think so,' he said as he pulled her back towards him and kissed her again. 'But work said they'd find me light duties if the surgeon gives me clearance, so I made an appointment with her for next Tuesday. I thought I'd hitch a lift to work and the hospital with you that morning. I checked your roster and you're on an early.'

'Sure,' Kitty said, just as her stomach rumbled.

Joe put his arm around her shoulder and led her into the apartment. 'And I also made dinner.'

'Dinner? How?' she said as she looked at his splinted arm.

'All right, I admit, I didn't make it but I ordered in. Indian takeaway. It's in the oven, keeping warm.'

'That's *our* dinner I can smell?'

'Yep. Butter chicken, rogan josh, garlic naan and rice.'

Kitty had eaten plenty of curries while she'd been pregnant. She'd found meat was more appetising when it was harder to recognise and she wondered if the baby would grow up with a taste for curry. 'You've been busy.'

Joe broke into a wide smile. 'Yep, but not too busy to avoid thinking about all the things we could do together when you got home.' He stepped behind her and kissed her earlobe as he slid his left hand under her shirt and cupped her breast.

Kitty's knees wobbled and heat pooled low in her belly as her nipple peaked under his fingers. She forgot about work. She forgot about the baby. Forgot about dinner and all her reservations about the future. She was only hungry for one thing now.

CHAPTER EIGHT

THE ED HAD been quiet today and Kitty was grateful. Even though it was almost three weeks since the assault she was still suffering from headaches and fatigue. The headaches weren't bad, just a dull ache behind her eyes at times, but she didn't like to take anything for the discomfort because of the baby. She was still trying to figure out if the fatigue was related to the concussion, the pregnancy or to the fact that she wasn't getting many early nights due to the combination of shift work and Joe's libido. She knew she was as much to blame as he was—she found him irresistible, and getting home to him was the highlight of her day.

She had dropped him at the ambulance station on her way to work this morning and arranged to meet him for lunch after his appointment with the hand surgeon. She'd been counting down the hours and hoping the department didn't experience a sudden influx of emergencies, eager to hear what the specialist had to say about Joe's proposed return to work.

He was getting bored and she hoped for his sake that he would be cleared for light duties but, from a purely selfish point of view, she was worried about how that would impact on her and on their fledgling relationship. In her mind it was the first step towards him getting his independence back, which might also prove to be the first nail in the coffin of their relationship. If he could work maybe he'd figure he could manage without her help. It was only a matter of time before he wouldn't need her as much any more. Maybe only a matter of time until he wouldn't need her at all.

'Kitty, Anna, incoming ambulance, two minutes.'

Her thoughts were interrupted by Davina, which was probably just as well, she figured as she made her way to the triage desk. She didn't want to dwell on the negatives, she needed to learn to be happy in the moment. She was trying but it didn't come naturally to her.

'Two-year-old toddler pulled from a back-yard pool,' the charge nurse told her and Anna as they gathered together. 'Resuscitated onsite.'

Kitty went pale. 'I can't do it, Davina,' she said. 'Please, can you find someone else?'

Davina knew her history. Kitty was always the last staff member called to these types of incidents.

'I'm sorry, Kitty. There isn't anyone else. I'll send someone to take over from you as soon as I can. Think of it as a seizure if it helps.'

But Kitty knew that wouldn't work. Treatment was different for a start. And once she'd heard the words 'pulled from a pool' her mind had gone straight to drowning and from there way back to her childhood.

Everyone in the emergency department had their own Achilles heel. Drowning or near-drowning incidents were Kitty's.

Anna handed Kitty a clean apron and put her arm around her shoulders. 'It'll be all right,' she told her. 'Just focus on me, I'll tell you what I need. You can do this.'

Kitty wasn't so sure, but it wasn't in her nature to let her colleagues or their patients down so she nodded and grabbed a fresh pair of gloves as she fought back a rising wave of nausea. She grabbed a blanket from the warming cupboard and followed Anna outside, hoping that the fresh air would clear her mind. Hoping Anna could get her through this.

The ambulance pulled into the bay and Kitty's first reaction was to look for Joe, before she remembered that he was still off work.

The paramedic who climbed out of the ambulance wasn't one Kitty knew. He pulled the stretcher out and spoke rapidly, giving Anna and Kitty the details he had.

'Twenty-six-month-old boy. Pulled from a private pool. Mother isn't sure how long he was immersed for but thinks it was less than ten minutes. Unresponsive. Respiratory and cardiac arrest. CPR was performed on-site. Resuscitated but unstable. Oxygen sats still low, eighty-six percent. Core temperature back up to thirty-six degrees.'

The child had a small oxygen mask over his nose and mouth, an IV line running into his arm and he was covered with a blanket to try to increase his body temperature slowly back to normal. Kitty draped the warmed blanket she carried over his inert body while some-how managing to keep her eyes averted.

'We'll need arterial blood gases and an FBE,' Anna said as they pushed the stretcher into the ED. 'And we'll need to intubate if his pulse ox doesn't improve.'

The little boy was listless, the edges of his lips tinged with blue.

Kitty tried not to look at him but it was im-possible as they transferred the child across to the exam couch. She could feel herself start-ing to shake. Black spots swam before her eyes and she thought she might be about to faint but then nausea swamped her, making her break out in a sweat. She grabbed a bowl from a trolley and vomited into it. She hadn't thrown up since she'd been hospitalised for concussion and before that it had been due to morning sickness, but she'd thrown up more in the past few months than in the rest of her entire life. But this was mental stress, not a physical thing.

'*Davina!*' Anna called out as the paramed-ics departed with their stretcher. 'I need some help in here.'

Davina came in and took one look at Kitty, who was standing motionless in the centre of the room, holding the plastic bowl in her hands.

'Kitty, go, take a break,' Davina instructed. 'I'll handle this.'

Kitty didn't waste any time getting out of there. She rinsed the bowl in the sluice room and headed for the change rooms. She opened her locker but ignored the salad she'd made for her lunch. She didn't think she could eat. She was still nauseous and shaky. She took her phone from her locker and pushed the button to speed-dial Joe.

'Hi, it's me,' she said when he answered. 'Can you meet me a bit earlier?'

'Sure. When?'

'Now.' She was close to tears. Hearing Joe's voice was almost enough to push her over the edge into hysteria. She needed to see him. She wanted his arms wrapped around her. It was the only thing that would make her feel safe.

'Is everything OK?'

She couldn't talk to him over the phone. She wanted to see him. Needed to feel him, to hear him tell her everything would be all right. 'I need to see you. Can you meet me in the ambulance bay?'

* * *

Kitty was sitting on the wall. She was hunched over, her elbows resting on her knees. She looked tiny. From this angle it was impossible to see her baby bump. She looked small and fragile. Wounded. Joe knew looks could be deceiving but he'd heard the tremor in her voice and he'd known instantly that something was wrong. He just didn't know what.

He could see her shoulders rise and fall—she was taking deep breaths. He reached out with his left hand, putting it on her shoulder. She jumped at his touch. She was shaking and he felt the coldness of her skin through the thin fabric of her scrubs. When she lifted her head, her eyes were dark, haunted, and a tell-tale crease of worry ran between her brows.

'Kitty, what is it? What's happened? Are you hurt?'

He ran his eyes over her but could see nothing.

She stood up, shaking her head, and stepped into his arms.

She fitted perfectly against his chest and he held her tight, as if his life depended on it. As if hers did.

'I'm worried about the baby.'

Joe frowned. He knew Kitty worried more than most people but, even so, something usually acted as a trigger for full-blown anxiety.

'What's going on?' he asked.

'The paramedics just brought in a two-year-old boy. A near-drowning.'

Now things started to make sense. Kitty used to be the middle one of three sisters. Her younger sister, Eliza, had drowned when she was two. Kitty had been almost six years old, and she'd never got over it. Her sister's death had been her first loss.

'It made me think of Eliza.'

'Of course it did,' Joe said as he rubbed her back. 'That's understandable.'

'But it also made me worry about all the other things that can and do go wrong. What if something happens to this baby?' She put her hand protectively over her belly.

'Kitty, you can't worry about unforeseen things.' He knew what she was like and he understood her concerns, but the reality was it wasn't going to be her job to worry about this baby once it was born. That would be Jess and Cam's responsibility. He knew Kitty sometimes forgot this baby wasn't hers to keep but he wasn't about to remind her of that right at this moment. 'I know you've suffered tragedies, but you need to stay positive.' He kept her in his embrace and led her away from the ambulance bay into the sunshine.

'Your body reacts to stress, the baby doesn't need that,' he said, trying to calm her and distract her by playing on her sense of responsibility to her unborn baby. He held her until she stopped shaking. 'Are you going to be OK?' he asked gently.

Her face was pale but he watched as she squared her shoulders and gave him a wan half-smile, nodding. 'Yes,' she answered as she stood up. 'I'll be fine. Thank you for being here.'

'I'll always be here,' he said as he kissed her forehead. As much as he wanted to follow her back into work, he couldn't go with her. He had to trust that she'd be all right. But his words echoed in his head as he watched her go. What exactly was he promising her? Would he always be there for her now? In what capacity? As a friend or a lover?

He didn't do serious commitment, but how could they go back now?

* * *

Kitty stretched her legs out in front of her and kicked her shoes off. She'd noticed her feet had started to swell at the end of her shifts and it felt good to have a day when she could put them up.

'What colour would you like?' Jess asked as she held out a selection of nail polishes. Cam had gone to play golf while Kitty visited Jess and they'd decided to spend the afternoon pampering themselves.

'That one,' Kitty said, choosing a pale pink.

'Is Joe working today?' Jess asked as she shook the little bottle before unscrewing the cap.

'Yes. This is his last week in the office. He should get the splint removed next week and he hopes then to be allowed back on the road as a spare.'

'Does that mean he'll be able to manage at home without you?'

'Mmm-hmm.'

'Has he asked you to stay?'

Kitty shook her head. 'No. There's no reason for me to stay once the splint comes off.' He wouldn't need her once the splint was removed, even though she'd be happy to stay.

It was ironic really—usually she was eager to be the one leaving before she could be left, but she and Joe were still in the early stages of their relationship and she was happy. She hadn't been really happy in a long time.

'How do you feel about that?' Jess asked. 'Were you hoping he would?'

'Yes.' Kitty answered honestly, avoiding eye contact with Jess whose head was bent over Kitty's feet as she painted her toenails. Kitty's pregnant bump made that impossible now. 'I was always planning on coming back here to you until the baby was born, and Joe knows that, but it would have been nice for him to ask. It would validate our relationship.'

She'd always planned on moving back in with Jess and Cam once Joe didn't need her help any more but she'd got used to their living—and sleeping—arrangements and she didn't actually want to leave.

'Maybe you should start the discussion,' Jess suggested, but Kitty shook her head.

Joe had said nothing. He'd given no hint as to where he thought their relationship might be heading. She shouldn't have been surprised, she knew he never got serious. It shouldn't upset her. It shouldn't bother her.

But it did. Their relationship felt right—perfect even—and she'd never felt like that before, about anyone. But she knew Joe didn't believe in perfect. He didn't believe in happily ever after. He wouldn't commit and she'd just have to accept that and hope that, at the end of the day, they could remain friends.

'Even if you move back here until the baby comes, where would you like to live once the baby is born? You'd be welcome to stay here, of course,' Jess offered as she started to cough.

'Thanks, but I don't think that's a good idea.' Kitty was starting to realise how hard it was going to be to relinquish the baby, and being in the same house would only make it more difficult. She needed to remember the baby wasn't hers, and that would be easier to do if she had some distance. 'You and Cam will need time with your baby by yourselves. Time to adjust to becoming a family.'

Jess was still coughing as Kitty finished speaking, so Kitty went to the kitchen to fetch a glass of water. Jess had had the cough for a while now and Kitty had been meaning to ask her about it but every time she started to, the conversation seemed to get redirected to talk of Joe or the baby or how Kitty was feeling. She'd ask her about it now, she decided as she filled the glass. Silence returned as she carried the drink back into the lounge. Jess had stopped coughing but was hunched over.

'Are you all right?' Kitty asked as she rubbed Jess's back.

Jess looked up. Her eyes were wide with fright and Kitty could hear her fighting to breathe.

'Oh, my God,' Kitty said. 'Is there something stuck in your throat?' she asked, knowing there couldn't be. They hadn't eaten. What was happening?

'Can you sit up?'

Jess shook her head. 'Hurts.'

Was she going blue around the lips? Surely she wouldn't deteriorate that quickly?

Kitty pulled her phone from her pocket and dialled 000.

'I need an ambulance. It's my sister. She can't breathe,' she said when she got through to Dispatch. 'No, there's no airway obstruction. I'm a nurse. Please hurry.'

Kitty put her phone on speaker while they waited, not wanting to be distracted. She boiled the kettle, wondering if warm, moist air would make breathing easier, before hurrying back into the lounge room. She didn't want to leave Jess alone. Her sister was fighting for air. Kitty placed two fingers on Jess's wrist, feeling for her pulse. Her touch met with rapid beats.

Please hurry. Kitty willed the ambulance to arrive but prepared herself to breathe for her sister.

'The ambulance is almost there.' The dispatcher's voice came through the phone. 'Can you hear the siren?'

'Yes.'

'OK. You can hang up now. Go and open the door for them.'

Kitty waited until the siren was switched off, indicating the ambulance was outside the front before she dared to leave Jess's side to open the door. 'This way,' she directed the paramedics. 'It's my sister. She's in respiratory distress.'

'Is she on any medication?'

'I don't know.' Kitty hated feeling so helpless. So useless. 'She's had treatment for ovarian cancer.'

'Has this happened before?'

'I don't think so.'

She made another phone call, this time to Cam, while the paramedics assessed Jess. She was almost in tears but knew she had to hold it together for a while longer. The paramedics might need more information from her.

The baby kicked in her belly and Kitty had the feeling she was reacting to her distress. Picking up on her emotions. She needed to remain calm. She put her hand protectively over her belly, as if trying to shield the baby from the drama. 'It's all right, little one,' she whispered. 'Your mum will be OK.'

As she made the promise to the baby she realised it was the first time she'd really acknowledged that her sister was the baby's mother. She'd said the words to others but had never said them out loud to herself. She had no idea if Jess would be OK, she had no idea if she was speaking the truth, but knew she was trying to calm herself as much as the unborn child. Jess *had* to be all right. Everyone needed her.

The paramedics had fitted an oxygen mask over Jess's face and were loading her onto a stretcher as Kitty made a second call to Joe. She grabbed her keys, her bag and Jess's handbag as she spoke to Joe. Keeping busy trying to do several things at once meant she didn't have time to fall apart.

She climbed into the front of the ambulance as Jess was loaded into the back and fretted as they negotiated the streets to the hospital.

The ambulance pulled into the bay at North Sydney. It felt surreal to be climbing out of the ambulance and walking into the ED as a family member. Kitty was used to being there as a nurse. She was used to having some control, used to it being her job to remain calm and to comfort, assess and treat patients and victims. She'd been a victim herself once after the assault but her recollection of that day was hazy at best. She had never presented to the ED as a family member before and having no control over the outcome, but all the worry, was hugely stressful.

She was relieved to see Anna and Victoria in the ambulance bay. She was on comfortable terms with Victoria again now that Kitty was the one sleeping with Joe. Victoria didn't seem to be holding any grudges.

She just had time to let them know that Jess was her sister before the paramedics pulled her from the ambulance and began to give Anna the rundown on Jess's condition.

Kitty followed Jess's stretcher into an exam room. She stood in a corner, out of the way. No one told her to leave and she figured if she was quiet no one would. She watched as Victoria replaced the oxygen tubing before strapping a blood-pressure cuff around Jess's arm and attaching the pulse oximetry monitor to her finger.

'Can you also put the ECG leads on?' Anna asked as she tightened the tourniquet and drew blood from Jess's arm. 'Did Jess have her chemo here?' she enquired. Kitty nodded. 'OK. Can you pull up her file?' Anna asked Victoria.

Victoria finished setting up the ECG and pushed the buttons to record Jess's cardiac rhythm before she went to the computer and pulled up her sister's electronic file. Kitty craned her neck but couldn't read the entries from where she stood.

Anna turned to look at her. 'She has metastases in her lungs?'

'What?' Kitty stepped forward, shaking her head. 'No. There must be another Jess McIntyre. Check the date of birth.'

Victoria read it out—the birthday matched, but the diagnosis didn't. 'No. There has to be a mistake.' Kitty reached for the edge of the barouche, steadying herself.

Anna double-checked the details. 'It's the right file,' she said. 'You didn't know?'

Kitty shook her head. *Secondaries!* The cancer had spread. Why didn't she know?

'We need to get a chest X-ray.'

Anna wasn't wasting time and she and Victoria wheeled Jess out of the room just as Cam arrived. Kitty could see the panic on his face. She expected she looked much the same.

'Where are they taking her?' he wanted to know.

'For an X-ray. Anna thinks she might have a blockage in her lung.' It was obvious to Kitty that Cam was nowhere near as surprised as she'd been by this news. 'You knew she had secondaries?'

Cam nodded.

'How long have you known?' Kitty was struggling with the fact that Jess's cancer had spread and yet no one had told her.

'We only got confirmation three weeks ago.'

'Three weeks! Why haven't you said anything?'

'That was Jess's decision.' Cam ran his fingers through his hair, making it even more dishevelled. 'She thought you had enough to worry about, and then she wanted you and Joe to have some time together where you could just focus on him and you. She knew you'd worry and want to move back in with us. She didn't want that.'

'What's her prognosis?' Kitty was almost afraid to ask. She already knew it wouldn't be good.

Cam's expression was dazed when he looked at her. He was probably in shock and perhaps it was unfair of her to grill him like this right now as he had a lot on his plate, but she had to know. They should never have kept this from her.

'The oncologist is talking weeks, a few months at best.'

Kitty sank onto a chair in the waiting room and wrapped her arms around her pregnant belly. She hadn't thought this day could get any worse. She'd been wrong.

Cam was crying now. Silent tears rolled down his cheeks. 'We're just hoping she'll be around to see the baby.'

'Has she been having treatment?'

Cam shook his head. 'There isn't anything they can do except for palliative options. Radiotherapy was suggested but Jess isn't keen.'

Kitty was stunned. Shocked. This seemed incomprehensible. 'I can't believe you didn't tell me.'

'I'm sorry, Kitty, but Jess insisted. She didn't want you to worry,' he said, just as Anna reappeared.

Kitty took a moment to register her return and another moment to realise Anna didn't know who Cam was. She stood up to introduce them. 'Anna, this is Cam, Jess's husband. Cam, this is Dr Lewis.'

'Is she all right?' Cam's question was abrupt. All sense of the social niceties had gone by the wayside, lost in the concern for his wife.

'She's OK.' *For now.* Kitty imagined Anna's unspoken words. 'She has a pleural effusion. I've called her oncologist and we're going to drain the fluid and hope that eases her breathing.'

'Can I see her?' Cam asked.

Anna nodded. 'Briefly.'

Cam followed Anna, leaving Kitty alone. Even the baby was quiet, which just served to heighten Kitty's sense of isolation. Was the baby asleep or in shock, like the rest of them? Kitty didn't know. She didn't know anything at the moment. She was swamped, drowning in emotion. She was worried for Jess but angry with her too. How could she have chosen not to tell her? *Why* had she chosen to keep this from her? Cam's explanation wasn't good enough. Jess was her sister. Kitty deserved to know.

She sank back down onto one of the plastic chairs, barely aware of how uncomfortable they were, and she was still sitting there, alone, when Joe arrived.

Kitty burst into tears when he walked through the door.

Joe rushed to her side and gathered her into his arms.

'What's happened?'

She knew he was expecting the worst and she fought back her tears long enough to tell him that the worst hadn't happened. Yet.

Cam came back just as Kitty finished updating Joe. His face was ghostly white.

Kitty stood up. Icy tendrils of alarm wrapped themselves around her heart but

Cam reassured her. 'She's OK. They're just about to try and drain the fluid.'

Joe stayed by Kitty's side, offering comfort, waiting until Jess's procedure was complete.

'That went well,' Anna said as she came back to where they waited. 'Jess is sleeping now. You'll be able to see her later.'

They continued to wait. Joe held Kitty's hand but they sat in silence. Kitty was lost in her own thoughts but took strength from Joe's presence. As always, he was there for her in a time of crisis.

Cam went to see Jess when she woke, and he was looking more relaxed when he returned to fetch Kitty. 'She's asking for you,' he said.

Jess was pale but seemed to be breathing more easily when Kitty entered the room. 'How are you feeling?' Jess looked better—she'd lost the blue tinge around her lips—and Kitty needed to know how she was. Any grievances Kitty had would have to wait, now was not the time to air them. 'Are you in a lot of pain?'

'No more than I have been for a while,' Jess replied.

'Cam said you could have radiotherapy. Why haven't you done that?'

'It's not a cure.'

'I know, but it might make you feel more comfortable.'

Jess gave a half-hearted smile. 'I thought I was managing. I wanted to wait until I really needed it. But my oncologist isn't giving me a choice now. She says I have to start treatment. The cough I can handle, but that feeling of not being able to breathe was terrifying. I don't want to go through that again if I can help it.'

'Good. If you can get your pain under control you'll feel better.' Kitty tried to focus on the practicalities, on what could actually be done, rather than the things that were out of their control. It wasn't easy. She topped up Jess's water glass before asking the question she really wanted answered. 'Why didn't you tell me?'

'I was going to,' Jess admitted, 'just not yet. I was trying to protect you and Cam.'

Kitty frowned. 'Cam said you only found out a few weeks ago. How could you protect him if you found out together?'

'The secondaries were only *confirmed*

three weeks ago but I'd been feeling off for a while before that.'

'And you didn't mention anything? Not even to Cam?'

Jess shook her head. 'You'd just had the implantation. I didn't want to stress anyone out, especially not you, with my concerns. I didn't want to risk anything going wrong. And I was worried that Cam might change his mind.'

'What—about the surrogacy?'

Jess nodded.

'Oh, Jess,' Kitty said as she clasped her sister's hand, 'I'm sure he wouldn't have. He adores you, he'd do anything for you. So would I.' Kitty wished, not for the first time, that she had someone in her life who adored her like Cam adored his wife.

Maybe she would still find that someone.

She didn't doubt that Joe loved her but only in the same way he always had. He'd not given her any indication that they were anything more than friends with benefits. It would never amount to anything more between them—not when Joe had no intention of committing to anyone. That was still what Kitty was aiming for, it had been what she'd always wanted, but until she was one hundred per cent sure that commitment was absolute, she wasn't going to give her heart away. She wanted to be loved, but it had to be for ever. And Joe didn't do for ever.

'I know,' Jess replied, 'but I thought the ethics committee and the doctors might not approve the surrogacy process if they suspected my health was deteriorating. And I was worried that if Cam thought I wasn't well enough he might change his mind, too. He may have wanted to focus on getting me better instead of on the pregnancy. But I'm not going to get better, so—'

'But you didn't know that at the time!' Kitty protested, interrupting her. 'Maybe if you'd done something earlier?'

'I could only handle one thing at a time, and having a baby was all I could think about. I want Cam to have something of me when I'm gone. I'm not feeling optimistic about this, and I had a feeling, a sixth sense, that things weren't good. The pregnancy gave me something to hold onto, something to look forward to.'

Kitty was crying now. Tears were rolling down her cheeks. She was hearing what Jess was telling her. She was going to lose her, too.

'Do you think I'm being selfish?' Jess asked.

'No. I would have done the same thing.' By offering to be their surrogate Kitty *had* done the exact same thing. Kitty understood all too well Jess's thought process. Family was important to both of them. Jess was only trying to give Cam a family of his own.

'You don't think having a baby will stop Cam from being able to find happiness later on?' Jess asked, leaving the rest of the sentence unspoken. Kitty didn't need to hear the words, *when I'm gone.* 'I am doing the right thing, aren't I?'

'Yes.' Kitty didn't want to make this any harder for Jess by burdening her with guilt. 'Is there anything I can do for you?'

'I don't like to ask, but do you think you could come home now? Just until the baby is born. I don't want to drag you away from Joe and I'll understand if you say no, but I feel like I'm missing out on the pregnancy and it's only a few more weeks. I don't want to miss another moment. I don't know how many more moments I'm going to get. But I'm planning to be around when my baby is born. I want to hold him, or her, in my arms.'

Kitty nodded. 'Of course, I'll come back,' she replied without hesitation. She would do anything for Jess, even if it meant giving up Joe for now. 'And it's a "her".'

'What?'

'You're having a daughter.'

'I am? Really?' Jess broke into a wide smile and Kitty realised then it had been a while since Jess had truly looked happy. How had Kitty not noticed that?

'Yes. Sorry, I know Cam wanted it to be a surprise but I wanted you to know.' Kitty refused to feel guilty about sharing that news. Who knew how long Jess had left? She should know the sex of her baby if that's what she wanted. Jess and Cam had kept the news of Jess's health from her and Kitty refused to be the one keeping secrets. It was up to Jess now to decide whether or not to share this news with Cam. 'I had an ultrasound at one of the student clinics and I asked them to tell me. It's a girl.'

Jess had tears in her eyes. 'Thank you,' she said just as the nurse came in to tell Kitty that Jess needed to rest.

Kitty hugged her sister and left the room. Joe was talking to Cam but he stopped and they both looked at her warily as she approached.

'What are you two discussing?' she asked.

Joe turned to her and Kitty noticed that Cam made himself scarce before Joe spoke. 'I think you should move back in with Jess and Cam,' he said. 'You'll worry if you stay with me. Jess needs you.'

Kitty wondered if Cam and Jess had already spoken about this or if Joe was making unilateral decisions. Regardless, she already knew that she needed to move back in with Jess. Kitty felt terrible that she hadn't noticed that Jess's health had been deteriorating. She'd worried that Jess was too thin and had worried about the cough but had never discussed it. Had she been too caught up in her own life, in her happiness with Joe, to notice? But that wasn't a good enough reason to have neglected her sister. She was family, and moving back to Jess and Cam's was the right thing to do. Kitty hadn't hesitated in agreeing with Jess just minutes earlier when she'd asked her to do exactly that, but hearing Joe suggest it was a little painful. She couldn't help but wonder if he wasn't a little too eager about the idea.

'Do you want to get rid of me?' she asked, only half-teasing.

Joe wrapped his arm around her and pulled her close. 'Not at all. But I know you will regret not spending this time with Jess.' He was right. Jess's time was limited. No one knew how long she had left, although nobody was brave enough to say that out loud. 'I've spoken with Cam and he agrees. It's just up to you.'

'But how will you manage?'

'I'll figure something out. My splint should be off next week and then if I'm back on the road as an extra crew member I won't be around much anyway.'

Was that a warning? Was he preparing her for what came next? She knew his relationships never lasted long. She knew he didn't do commitment. Had he had enough?

This was exactly why she always walked away first. So that she wouldn't have this feeling of betrayal and loss. It was all too much, but she couldn't face dealing with that now. Jess needed her and Kitty wasn't about to let her down. She needed to let Joe go, needed to prioritise what was important, but she couldn't help thinking about the things Joe hadn't said. She couldn't stop thinking of all the things that could go wrong. Not with Jess but between her and Joe. Was this the first step towards the end?

Joe had been trying to do the right thing, sending Kitty back to live with Jess and Cam, but he'd barely seen her for the past four weeks, and there were still three weeks to go until the baby was due. Not that it would change things—Joe knew Kitty would stay with her sister for as long as she could. Until the end.

He knew he was being ridiculous, he understood the situation. Jess was the only family she had left, their time was limited, and he knew how much family meant to Kitty. Still, it hurt that she seemed to have so little time left for him, and he was surprised how keenly he was feeling her absence. He missed her. He had enjoyed the change in their relationship. But he wasn't family and he also knew that if he wanted to be a priority for her he would have to make promises that he wasn't sure he could keep.

And he couldn't do that.

He couldn't give her what she wanted,

and he knew that meant he would lose her. Eventually she would choose someone else, a man who could offer her all the things she wanted—love, a future, a family of her own. *Commitment.*

He couldn't be that man.

He would have to let her go.

CHAPTER NINE

'ALL RIGHT, KITTY, you're doing well. I can see the baby's head. You can push with the next contraction.'

Kitty had had no idea childbirth would be this painful, but her labour had progressed quickly for a first-time mum and now it was almost over. She hoped. She was concentrating hard. Thinking about the moment the baby would be put into her arms. It stopped her from thinking about the pain.

'You can do this, Kitty.'

'You're almost there.'

Cam stood on one side of her, Jess sat on the other. Jess wasn't strong enough to stand throughout the delivery but Kitty was relieved that she was going to be able to hold her baby. She'd been determined to make that happen for Jess, and the pain she was experiencing was a small price to pay for her sister's happiness.

Kitty knew that Joe was waiting outside the door. Cam had called him when she'd gone into labour. He'd wanted to know and Kitty was happy for him to be told, but she didn't want him in the delivery room. She needed her energy to focus on the people who were truly invested in this.

'All right, Kitty, push. That's it,' the obstetrician instructed as another contraction gripped her abdomen. She felt as though she was being crushed like a car at the wrecker's yard but she pushed with everything she had. The sooner she delivered this baby the sooner she'd get to rest. 'OK, hold it there.'

Kitty stopped pushing and panted. Jess was talking to her but Kitty couldn't really understand what she was saying. She was tired and sore and all her focus was concentrated below her waist, which didn't leave any room in her head for conversation.

'Nearly there, Kitty. One last time. Push.'

Kitty squeezed Jess and Cam's hands tight and, leaning forward, she pushed hard. She felt the release as she pushed the baby out of her body and she breathed out as she heard the newborn cries.

'Congratulations, everyone,' said the obstetrician, 'you have a healthy baby girl.'

Kitty watched in almost a dream-like trance as the baby was passed to her. The midwife loosened Kitty's gown at the neck so that she could rest on Kitty's chest, skin to skin, and the baby quietened as soon as she felt that contact.

Jess reached out and slid her finger into the palm of the baby's hand and smiled.

'Cameron, are you going to cut the cord?' the midwife asked as she clamped the cord and handed Cam the scissors.

Cam did the honours and the midwife took the baby and swaddled her before handing her to Jess.

They were a family.

A family Kitty had helped them to create. An achievement that should make her proud and happy but there was underlying sadness too. She felt the loss immediately but tried to smile and say all the right things as she watched Jess and Cam cuddle her baby.

No, not her baby. Their daughter. Eliza Kate. The baby was being named for Jess's two sisters—Eliza and Kitty—but she would be Lizzie for short.

Kitty had given them this gift—a family of their own—but she wasn't quite ready to let go. It was much harder than she'd imagined. And she didn't *want* to let go. Of anyone. Not of Lizzie, and not of Jess.

And what about Joe?

Joe had given her space, time to spend with Jess, but she missed him. He'd checked on her, called her, told her he was there for her, but she missed him physically. Her body missed him. She appreciated that he was offering emotional support but she wanted more now. She wanted everything, but she knew he couldn't give her that. She knew their relationship was changing—*had* changed. She'd understood it would have a use-by date, that was how Joe operated. She just didn't know if she was prepared for that. He was her best friend, her lover, but he couldn't—or wouldn't—be her partner, and she knew eventually she'd have to let him go. Or that he would leave.

She wiped a tear from the corner of her eye. She couldn't think about Joe right now. Lizzie and Jess needed her.

* * *

Joe was worried about Kitty. He'd visited her in hospital every day since she'd given birth and he knew something wasn't right. Jess had been with Kitty almost every time Joe had visited and despite the fact that Jess was terminally ill and looked tired and frail, she at least looked happy. Kitty did not.

He'd known she would find the first few days post-partum difficult. He knew she would miss being pregnant, would miss being the mother of her baby, and he was worried that, in a way, she would perceive it as yet another loss. He'd seen the sadness in the depths of her dark eyes and he wanted to eradicate it, but he was having difficulty finding the right words. He wanted to be there for her, to offer his unwavering support, as he always had. He wanted to put a smile on her face, to promise her that her future would be bright and happy and everything she dreamed of, but the words kept getting stuck in his throat.

He knocked quietly on the open door of her room, not wanting to disturb her if she was sleeping, but she was awake. She was feeding the baby, watching her as she suckled, and she didn't hear him come into the room.

She looked so peaceful. Joe was taken aback. He hadn't thought about what would happen after the baby was born. He'd assumed the baby would be bottle fed, but once he'd got over his surprise he had to admit to himself that he liked to see Kitty mothering the baby.

He stood rooted to the spot as a wave of emotion flooded him. What if that was *his* baby she was holding?

The idea filled him with a longing that was almost painful. For the first time in his life he could picture a future that had more than him, alone in the frame. What if this was his future? Kitty, and a family of their own?

He was still standing stunned and mesmerised in the doorway when Kitty looked up and saw him.

'Hi. You have perfect timing,' she said as she took Lizzie from her breast and pulled her top down. Watching her, Joe felt another pang of longing. Not sexual but visceral. He wanted Kitty. He wanted to make her his. He didn't want to live without her. *Couldn't* live without her. 'Would you mind holding Lizzie while I have a shower?'

She got out of bed and handed the baby to him without waiting for his answer, completely unaware of the thoughts racing through his head.

He looked down at the tiny bundle that was swaddled in his arms and imagined she was his and Kitty's. He knew then that this was what he wanted. He wanted Kitty to have his babies. He wanted to be part of her entire life. He wanted to feel her swollen, pregnant belly and know that part of him was within her.

'I can't put her straight down after a feed,' Kitty was saying, 'and I need to get ready.'

'Ready for what?' he asked.

'I'm going home today.'

'Home?'

'To Jess and Cam's. I'm going to express milk for Lizzie and it makes sense to all be together. Lizzie has to live with Cam and Jess for at least thirty days before they can apply to transfer her parentage.'

Joe had seen Jess; he wasn't sure that she'd last that long.

'They don't want time together, just the three of them?' he asked, but as soon as the words were out of his mouth he could tell by Kitty's expression that he'd upset her. He knew she thought he was implying she wouldn't be welcome. He started to tell her that wasn't what he'd meant but Kitty was already talking.

'Jess needs me there.' Kitty's voice was tight. She was definitely upset and her eyes were still dark, haunted by pain and loss. 'She won't be able to manage on her own, she's not well enough. I'm not there just to help with Lizzie, I'm going to be Jess's palliative care nurse. Jess wants to spend time with her family and that includes me.'

Joe's heart ached for Kitty and for all the people she had lost and was yet to lose. His heart ached for her future. And for his. For all the things he couldn't give her back. Was she leaving him before he could leave her?

He hadn't seen that coming. He'd assumed they'd be able to sort things out, but it seemed he'd been naïve. He would lose Kitty unless he could show her he could be the man she needed.

He loved her, and he wanted to build a future with her. A future and a family of their own—and he knew there was only one way to make that happen.

Kitty's life had become one long series of appointments. She seemed to spend her days waiting. Waiting for the paediatrician, the obstetrician, the oncologist, and waiting for Jess to have her radiotherapy sessions. But it wasn't helping.

Kitty didn't want to admit it but she was waiting for Jess to die. They all were. Jess was struggling more every day. Struggling with the pain, struggling to breathe, struggling to talk and struggling to eat. She was fading before Kitty's eyes and Kitty didn't think she could bear it. The only time Jess looked at peace was when she was holding her daughter.

Yesterday's appointment had at least been something a bit different. They'd been to court and Lizzie's parentage had been transferred from Kitty to Cam and Jess. Kitty was no longer officially Lizzie's mother. Jess had got her wish—she had her daughter.

But Kitty was scared now about what that meant. She knew that this was what Jess had been waiting for. Her sister had been barely holding on. All that had kept her going were the milestones she had created to tick off. One—the surrogacy. Two—waiting for Lizzie. Three—waiting to officially become Lizzie's mother. And now she'd achieved all those things. She was a mother. Jess had given Cam his daughter, created a family. And now she could say goodbye.

Kitty's knees buckled as Jess's coffin was lowered into the ground. Joe's arm tightened around her waist, supporting her, offering comfort, but he wasn't sure she was even aware of his presence. She certainly hadn't turned to him for support after Jess had died just over a week ago. Kitty had just locked herself away with Cam and the baby, and Joe was beginning to think she was lost to him for ever. She seemed to have cut Joe out of her life without warning.

Kitty had gone through the entire funeral service without making a sound. She'd cried fat silent tears and had hugged people and nodded in reply to their condolences, but she hadn't spoken a word.

She had looked at Joe when he'd offered to drive her to the cemetery and he'd almost expected her to refuse him, but she'd wordlessly followed him to his car and sat silently beside him for the short trip. Cam and Lizzie were being driven by Cam's parents, who had come down to Sydney from northern New South

Wales and Joe was grateful to have Kitty to himself. But what he hadn't expected was the hollow, fragile shell of a woman who sat beside him. She'd lost weight in the past few weeks, and it was more than just the pregnancy weight. Her face had lost some of its usual roundness, her eyes were dark with grief, and her cheeks were hollow and pale. She was a shadow of her normal self.

He had the impression that Kitty was only just holding it together. He kept his arm around her, anchoring her to the ground, anchoring her to him as Cam handed his six-week-old daughter to his mother and stepped forward. He bent down to scoop a handful of dirt from the mound at his feet and Joe watched his lips move as he bade his wife goodbye quietly before he opened his fingers and let the earth fall into the grave.

Cam turned back to his parents and his daughter. He had his family, but Kitty had no one, and Joe's heart ached for her.

Kitty sobbed and turned her face in against Joe's shoulder as the sound of the dirt hitting the coffin echoed in the hole. He didn't know if she was aware she was leaning on him but he wasn't going to abandon her. She had shut him out for the past six weeks, refusing to step out of the house unless it was to accompany Jess somewhere, but, as pathetic as it made him seem, he would still take any opportunity he could get to have her in his arms. He knew she felt alone, and seeing Jess being buried beside her parents and younger sister would only reinforce that. But Kitty had him. She'd always have him and he would be there for her. He knew she would need him again.

The mourners had all begun to make their way, in silence, back to their cars, but Kitty hadn't moved. She was standing still, staring at the ground.

Joe didn't know if she had seen everyone starting to leave. They were all going back to Cam's house for the wake. He didn't know if Kitty intended on going back there but, then again, where else would she go? That was where she was living.

'Kitty?'

'Can you give me a minute?' she said as she pulled away from him.

He let her go. She might have been standing a few inches away from him but emotionally he felt as though there was a chasm separating them. He couldn't remember the last time he'd seen her smile, heard her laugh. He missed her, desperately. The light inside her had dimmed and his heart ached for her and everything, everyone, she'd lost.

He needed her back. He needed to reach out, build a bridge over that chasm and get her back. For her sake and his.

He watched and waited as she went to each of the other graves—her mother's, her father's, her baby sister's. Joe could see fresh flowers at the base of their gravestones and he realised Kitty had already visited the cemetery today. She must have placed the flowers there.

He watched from a distance as she bent and took a flower from each grave. She hadn't asked for his support, but he still waited and watched, feeling as if his heart might break. Kitty had always seemed fragile and he was worried that Jess's death might be the final straw. The thing that would finally break her. He would do anything to protect her but he had never felt so useless. All he could do was to stay close by, to be there if she needed him.

She sank onto the ground, kneeling beside the freshly dug grave and, one by one, she dropped each flower into the hole to land on Jess's coffin.

She sat quietly for a few minutes before eventually standing and coming back to Joe. Her eyes were red-rimmed.

'Shall we go?' he asked as he took a freshly laundered handkerchief from his pocket and handed it to her.

He didn't ask if she was ready to leave. He didn't ask if she was OK. He knew she was neither of those things but she couldn't stay here for ever. Everyone would be expecting her back at Cam's house. She may not want to speak to anyone, and if that was the case Joe would protect her, shield her, make excuses for her, but he knew she would want to be close to Lizzie. It would make her feel connected to Jess.

She nodded and let him take her hand.

He drove her to Cam's house and did all the things that no one else had the energy to manage. He provided endless cups of tea and coffee, spoke to the caterers, topped up people's drinks and tidied away dirty dishes.

Having baby Lizzie there was a good distraction but Joe could see Kitty getting antsy as Cam's mother monopolised the baby. Joe couldn't blame her. Lizzie was her first, and probably only, grandchild, but he knew that Kitty felt a connection that no one else did when it came to the baby.

As Cam and Jess's friends started to leave, Joe managed to persuade Kitty to go for a walk with him. He thought she might need some space, and he needed to talk to her. They didn't get further than the park down the street, but sitting on the park bench in the quiet of twilight gave them a chance to talk without interruption.

'Cam's father told me they're planning on staying in Sydney for a while to give Cam a hand,' he said as he sat beside Kitty. 'What are your plans?' He kept his gaze fixed on a gum tree in the distance, unfocussed and non-confrontational, as he asked his question.

'I can't make plans,' Kitty replied flatly. She sounded upset and confused and he was worried about her. He knew she struggled to cope with situations like this—losing people she loved.

'You're welcome to move back in with me if you like. Let Cam have some time with his family and the baby?'

'I'm his family too,' she replied. 'I'm Lizzie's mother.'

'You're her *aunt*, Kitty.' He knew the paperwork had been signed, officially transferring Lizzie's parentage to Cam and Jess. Kitty was Lizzie's birth mother but she had no claim on her now.

Kitty was shaking her head. 'I can't leave the baby. She's all I have left.'

Joe should have seen this coming. He knew Kitty had a fear of being abandoned herself. She'd lost first her younger sister, then her parents, and now Jess. He knew she saw the baby as a part of her. In a way, the baby *was* a part of her—but not one she got to keep. He couldn't believe no one had seen this coming. Wasn't this the sort of thing that should have been anticipated from the counselling sessions prior to the surrogacy? He could understand how a baby would satisfy Kitty's need to have someone to love, to have someone who wouldn't leave her. Was it any wonder she was having difficulty letting Lizzie go? But Lizzie wasn't the child that would fix all this. Kitty needed to move on. She needed to create a life for herself. A family for herself. She didn't get to keep Jess's.

'I understand you're sad, Kitty, I know you're hurting, but you can't be a substitute for Jess. Cam and Lizzie were *her* life. *Her* family. You need to have your own.'

'I know you think you understand, Joe, but you don't know what it's like to lose everybody. I can't let them go too.'

'I can help you, Kitty. Come home with me.'

'Please don't make this about you, Joe. I can't think about you at the moment.' She stood up from the bench and started walking.

Joe walked with her, in silence. He couldn't let her go alone, but who was he to say she was wrong about him not understanding what it was like. One thing Joe knew he did understand was *her*, but he couldn't stop the feeling that Kitty was removing herself emotionally from him. He'd always been there for her, available to pick up the pieces, but maybe she didn't want that any more.

Maybe she didn't want him.

She was walking away but he wasn't prepared to let her go. He couldn't. She was upset but he couldn't, he *wouldn't*, abandon her. He knew that was her greatest fear and he wasn't about to leave her too. But he knew it wasn't only up to him.

If Kitty chose to walk away there wasn't much he could do.

Kitty missed Joe, but she was trying desperately to hold onto her family, or what she had left of them. She missed him terribly but she couldn't bring herself to abandon Lizzie and Cam. She needed them and she was certain they needed her. They would always be family. In her mind that meant they were there to stay. *Until death do us part.* She'd only been parted from the rest of her family by death. She would hold onto them with everything she had. Even if that meant giving up Joe. He didn't need her. Not like Lizzie did. She needed to stay strong for Lizzie.

Normally she would have relied on Joe to give her that strength, but she didn't want to depend on him now. He wouldn't be there for her for ever. For ever was a long time. Eventually she would have to manage without him, and she should start getting used to it now. Their relationship wasn't serious. It wasn't ever going to last. He would never commit— she knew they wanted different things in life, and she couldn't expect him to hang around. At some point he'd grow bored with her, or see something better. He'd told her that's exactly what his parents did and he was convinced he was cut from the same cloth. Kitty had no reason to doubt him. As long as she'd known him he'd never had a long-term relationship.

Neither had she.

She'd ruined their friendship by sleeping with him, but she couldn't deal with that reality along with Jess's death. She had to put Joe to one side. She'd deal with the consequences later, when she was stronger.

She missed him but she didn't want to see him.

Every time she did she had to fight the urge to run into his arms. Every time she saw him, it felt like her heart was breaking and then she had to start the whole process of getting over him again. She wasn't sure what hurt more—losing Jess or losing Joe—but she had no choice. She knew she had deliberately cut him out of her life, but she figured that eventually the pain would ease. She was hoping so.

This heartache would pass. It had to.

She bent her head to kiss the soft, downy hair on Lizzie's head. She breathed in the baby smell as she rearranged her clothes. She had been breastfeeding Lizzie but the baby had now fallen asleep and Kitty need to put her back in her bassinette. No one knew she was still breastfeeding. She was expressing milk so that Cam could feed his daughter too but Kitty loved the closeness she felt when she was feeding Lizzie and she didn't want to give that up, so she volunteered for the midnight feed when the house was quiet and she and Lizzie could have their moment. She whispered her thoughts to Lizzie at the same time.

She couldn't talk to Jess. Or to Joe. The closest she had to a confidante now was this little baby. Lizzie was only ten weeks old, hardly a substitute for Joe or Jess, but she was the next best thing. This was bonding time for the two of them. She wasn't officially the baby's mother any more, but she was the closest thing to a mother that tiny Lizzie had.

Unless, or until, Cam remarried.

Kitty couldn't stand the idea of Cam replacing Jess, but she knew it was ultimately a possibility. Cam was only young. He had the rest of his life in front of him.

Kitty wiped a tear away. She was crying for everyone she'd lost. Including Joe.

She stood up to wrap Lizzie and tuck her into her bassinette. She didn't want to think about Joe. She didn't have the energy. Cam *might* replace Jess, but Joe would *surely* replace Kitty, and she didn't want to think about how that would make her feel. There was only so much she could handle at the moment, and that didn't include thinking about her relationship with Joe.

She knew she had pushed him away. She'd been scared of losing him but she'd gone and done it anyway, just as Jess had warned her, leaving her more miserable and even lonelier than before.

CHAPTER TEN

KITTY HAD RETURNED to work but she still hadn't moved out of Cam's house. Joe had no idea how long she was planning to stay there. Did she have any intention of leaving? He didn't know, but he knew she was avoiding him. The only time he saw her was when they were at work. She was a shadow of her former self—her wide smile was absent, her dimples gone, her curves shrunk. She'd shut down completely and shut him out.

He'd called around to Cam's house—he refused to think of it as Kitty's even though she still lived there—several times, checking on them both, wanting to make sure they were coping. He'd tried to time it around Kitty's days off, wanting to see her, but every time he'd visited she'd made an excuse and avoided him.

But Joe was refusing to give her up.

She'd made a decision but he wasn't going to sit back and let her throw away their relationship. She was too important to him. Their *future* was too important to him.

So he'd enlisted Cam's help in order to see Kitty. That had been a major exercise in subterfuge. He'd had to anticipate her every rebuttal and plan a response. He had to co-ordinate with Cam to make sure someone was home to look after Lizzie so Kitty didn't have that excuse, and he had to make sure Kitty wasn't either at work or asleep.

He knocked on Cam's front door and invited her to brunch. 'There's something I need to tell you,' he said, hoping her curiosity would outweigh any reluctance.

'Now is not a good time, Joe.'

He could tell from her voice that something had upset her and immediately his protective instincts kicked into gear. If Kitty needed him he planned on being there for her, and this time he wasn't going to let her fob him off.

'Come for a walk with me to the beach then. Talk to me. Tell me what's going on.' Maybe walking would be better than sitting at a café. There would be no one to overhear them and Kitty wouldn't feel as if he was cross-examining her.

She hesitated, and he was preparing his speech to plead his case when she surprised him be agreeing. 'OK.'

He waited while she found her shoes and her keys. He heard her tell Cam she was going for a walk and would be back soon.

'Tell me what's happened,' Joe said as they hit the sand.

'Cam had a letter from the fertility clinic asking him what he wants to do with the remaining frozen embryos.'

Joe hadn't realised there were surplus ones. 'What are his options?'

'He can destroy them, donate them to a couple who need them or he could keep them and use them.'

'What does he want to do?'

As Joe asked the question he realised what the issue could be. Why Kitty was upset. Was Cam's decision not the one Kitty wanted? Joe fought off a wave of panic—was Kitty thinking about offering to be a surrogate again? He knew she'd want to have as much of Jess as possible, which could include another baby, but if she went down this path again she was effectively putting her own life on hold once more and to Joe, that meant his life as well. He loved her but was he prepared to wait for ever?

His heart was in his mouth as he asked, 'What do *you* want, Kitty?'

That was the crux of the matter. What did Kitty want?

A life with him or a life with her sister's children?

She had to choose. He had to offer her a choice, and she had to make it.

Kitty had missed Joe. She'd missed everything about him. His kindness, his smile, his hands on her body, his lips on hers, his ability to listen without judging, his ability to make her feel better. It felt good to be back by his side. To confide in him.

She wanted to slide her hand into his as they walked. She wanted to feel connected to another person, but she wasn't sure if they had that relationship any more. She wasn't sure what they'd done to their friendship. Had they completely destroyed it? Had she?

She shoved her hands into the pockets of

her shorts instead and kept pace alongside him on the sand.

He'd asked her what she wanted.

'I want my family back,' she replied honestly, knowing it was an impossible wish.

'Kitty...'

'It's all right,' she said, pre-empting his reply, 'I know it's not possible but it's what I want.'

'And is that why you're still living with Cam?' he asked. 'Are they your family now? Is that what you want? Jess's family?'

'They are my family too,' she protested. He couldn't begrudge her that. 'Lizzie needs me.'

'I'm not disagreeing with that, but she is not your daughter. She is Cameron's daughter. Your sister's daughter. She is your niece. And you love her, as you should, but you should have daughters of your own. A family of your own. I know you want that.'

But that was the problem. She shook her head. 'It's not going to happen for me. Everyone always leaves me.'

'*I* can make it happen.'

'You?'

'Yes. Me. Where do I fit into your life? Is there room for me? For us?'

'Us? Is there an "us"?'

'Of course there is. Nothing's changed.'

She should be pleased to hear that. She'd been worried that he would cast her aside, move on, but in a sense this was what she'd really feared. That nothing had changed. And she didn't want that. She didn't want to be just friends. She wanted more. She loved him but she wanted her happily ever after, and she wasn't going to get that from Joe.

He stopped walking and turned towards her. His face was serious, his blue eyes earnest. 'You deserve to find your own happiness. With someone who loves you. You deserve a family of your own, a husband and children of your own, and I want to give it to you. You should be with me.'

'What are you saying?' She wasn't sure she understood.

'I promised I would always be there for you. I was there for you when your parents died, when Jess died... But I don't just want to be there for you when things go wrong. I want to be there for you always. I want to be the one standing beside you in the good times *and* the bad. I love you, Kitty, and I want to give you a family of your own. A family with me. Let us build the life we want together. Marry me.'

'But you don't want to get married.'

'I do.' He reached out and took both her hands in his. Her racing heart slowed and calmed with his touch. She'd missed that, and she didn't ever want him to let her go. 'I was worried I couldn't give you what you needed most—commitment—but the past few months have shown me that I want to try. I know you are the woman for me. You always have been, but the last few months have shown me just how much better my life is with you in it, how much happier I am. I've missed you with every piece of me and I will do everything I can to make this work. I want to marry you. I only intend to get married once, I intend to do it right, and with you I know I've got it right. We can do this. Together. I know I can be the man you need. I need to know if I am the man you want.'

She loved him, desperately, but she didn't know if she could do this. 'I'm scared, Joe.'

'Of what?'

'Of losing you.' She'd lost everyone she'd ever loved and she couldn't bear to lose him too. Her heart couldn't stand it. She'd lost too many people already.

But you love him. I know you do.

Jess's voice was in her head and Kitty knew what she'd be saying if she was standing beside her. She could hear the words.

You have to make a choice. You can love him now and take a chance or you can send him away and know you're losing him for certain. Make your choice but there's only one choice that might give you the happiness you crave. The happiness you deserve. He's a good man and he loves you.

'I love you.' Joe's voice blended with the voice in her head. Jess and Joe, the two people she loved more than anyone else, were telling her the same thing.

But only one of them was still here.

He continued speaking. 'I've never wanted to make a commitment because I thought I would never find the right person. What I didn't realise was the right person was in front of me all along. That person is you, Kitty. I want to be beside you, I want to spend the rest of my life with you,' he told her. 'My parents were always looking for their next partner, they were never happy with what they had, but I'm always and only looking for you. I can't be truly happy without you and I want to spend the rest of my life showing you how I feel. Being yours. If you'll have me.'

'You won't leave me?'

'Never.'

Kitty was crying now.

'Do you love me?' Joe asked.

Kitty nodded. 'Yes. I do.'

Joe dropped to one knee in the sand, their hands entwined, their fingers interlaced. 'Kitty, I love you with every part of me. I want to share my life with you, for eternity. I promise to love you and adore you and never leave you. I want to make you happy, to make you laugh. I want to share my life with you as more than friends. I want us to be partners, lovers, parents to our children. I want us to be a family. I love you and I want to be your husband. Please, will you be my wife? Will you marry me?'

Kitty had to make a choice. She had to take a chance. If she didn't she would lose everything.

She'd already lost too much.

She would take the chance. She would choose the man she loved.

She had loved him for years and she didn't want to live without him. She needed him, but she wanted him too. He was her best friend, her lover and she wanted him to be her husband. She wanted him to give her a family of her own. She believed him when he promised never to leave her, for he'd always been there for her when she'd needed him. He had *already* proved that he could commit to her. She trusted him—and she loved him.

She tugged on his hands and pulled him to his feet. She wiped a tear from her eye but she knew he'd know the tears were happy ones. He knew her so well. And if he didn't, then the ridiculous smile on her face would surely have shown him how she felt.

'I love you,' she said as she wrapped her arms around his neck and pulled him close, 'and I want to spend the rest of my life with you.'

He bent his head until his lips brushed hers. 'Is that a yes?' he whispered.

Kitty nodded. 'Yes, my love, I will marry you. I promise to love you always, to be your family, your wife and the mother of your children, now and for ever.'

Joe wiped the tear from her cheek and

kissed her again and in that kiss she could taste his promises and his love and, finally, she was complete.

* * * * *

If you enjoyed this story, check out these other great reads from Emily Forbes

**ONE NIGHT THAT CHANGED HER LIFE
A MOTHER TO MAKE A FAMILY
WAKING UP TO DR. GORGEOUS
FALLING FOR THE SINGLE DAD**

All available now!